Christian Bend

ADVANCE PRAISE

Christian Bend is a beautifully vivid and authentic rendering of Appalachia. Karen Spears Zacharias grabs us by the heart and doesn't let go—it's all here in *Christian Bend*: tragedy, love, redemption, spirituality, and beauty. Zacharias knows how to catch the language, cadence, and intricacy of mountain life in the net of her engrossing story; she never averts her gaze from the terrible or the wonderful. Zacharias introduces us to a wide cast of characters with varied voices and then seamlessly connects them all in ways both stunning and unexpected. We find Burdy Luttrell recovering from a gunshot wound, and from there the mystery of not only the shooting but also Burdy's hidden life blooms in this page-turning novel.
—Patti Callahan Henry, *New York Times* best-selling author

With stunning beauty and more twists and turns than a Tennessee mountain road, Karen Spears Zacharias's novel *Christian Bend* takes readers on an unforgettable journey through the gamut of human emotion, ultimately illuminating the meaning and necessity of forgiveness in our lives. Literary fiction worth its salt should speak to the human condition, or at least attempt to do so. *Christian Bend* does not disappoint and will leave you on your feet, tears streaking your face, cheering for more.
—Michel Stone, award-winning author of *Border Child* and *The Iguana Tree*

In language rich and specific, Karen Spears Zacharias summons the mountains—its hymns and spells, its trees flaming with reds and golds, its families and their secrets. But Christian Bend, Tennessee is also part of a new culture of drugs, addiction and violence—a changing landscape. Coaxing beauty from the hollers of both memory and present, *Christian Bend* reminds us of the importance of place and of spirit. Some visions, Zacharias tells us, are meant to be heeded.
—Karen Salyer McElmurra,

MERCER UNIVERSITY PRESS

Endowed by

TOM WATSON BROWN
and
THE WATSON-BROWN FOUNDATION, INC.

Christian Bend

A Novel

Karen Spears Zacharias

Mercer University Press | MACON, GEORGIA

2017

MUP/ P548

Published by Mercer University Press
1400 Coleman Avenue
Macon, Georgia 31207

9 8 7 6 5 4 3 2 1

Books published by Mercer University Press are printed on acid-free
paper that meets the requirements of the American National
Standard for Information Sciences—Permanence of Paper for
Printed Library Materials.

ISBN   978-0-88146-623-2
Cataloging-in-Publication Data is available from the Library of
Congress

PREVIOUS WORKS

Burdy (Mercer University Press)

Mother of Rain (Mercer University Press)

Karly Sheehan: The True Crime behind Karly's Law (Redbird)

Will Jesus Buy Me a Double-Wide? (Zondervan)

Where's Your Jesus Now? (Zondervan)

After the Flag Has Been Folded (William Morrow)

Benched: The Memoirs of Judge Rufe McCombs (Mercer

   University Press)

The alienated must seek forever the means of reentry
into the world of man.

—*Agnes "Sissy" Grinstead Anderson*

With Great Love for

Lucille Shropshire Christian (Aunt Cil)

Lon Christian (Cousin Lon)

&

the community of Christian Bend, Tennessee

CHRISTIAN BEND

Chapter 1

He woke in his mother's bed. His head as heavy as an iron mallet. A dried-out bottle of Jack Daniels overturned on the bedside table next to his grandmomma's Bible, the one Maizee had brung with her to the Bend all those many years ago. A pack of dogs was howling in the distance. Mosely's beagles had likely treed a coon up on the slope behind the house.

Rain eased his long legs off the side of the bed and sat up gingerly, careful not to jerk his head to one side or the other. Cautious, too, of not erupting the burning in his belly. Hunching over, he tried to remember how he come to be in his momma's bed. Rain hadn't been in his parents' bedroom since the day Doc and Leela-Ma sat in the basement of the church and, using felt-board pictures, explained to his four-year-old deaf self that his momma had died and gone to be with Jesus. Years passed before he learned the gruesome way Maizee had died.

On that faraway day, they'd all come to the house together, Doc carrying young Rain the entire time as Leela-Ma packed up the boy's belongings. Doc had tried to put the child down when they first entered the house.

"Sit here on the couch while I help your Aunt Leela," Doc instructed. Rain couldn't make out what Doc was saying, but the minute Doc leaned over the davenport to sit the toddler down, Rain dug into his uncle's neck, locked his feet around the crook of Doc's elbows, and let loose a wail that had Con Christian telling anybody who passed his house for the next month that he'd heard Gabriel's trumpet, sure enough. So Doc held the boy while Leela-Ma gath-

1

ered his belongings and stuffed them in a suitcase she'd pulled out from underneath the bed.

From then on, Rain's best memories, the ones that made him smile to himself, always had Doc and Leela in the smack-dab middle. While he never called them anything but Doc and Leela-Ma even now, Rain thought of them the way a boy does his parents. Throughout his life, Doc and Leela were Rain's source of security. It was their advice he sought in the troubling times of life, and in the everyday matters, too.

But on this late Monday morning (afternoon, if truth be told), Rain found himself doubting Doc and Leela's motives for the very first time. Had they known Burdy's secret? Kept it from him all these years?

"Aww, crap," Rain said, standing up in the boots he had not removed before passing out sometime before the sun popped up over the hills.

He reeked like a field hand after a Saturday night binge. He'd drunk so much Jack Daniels he was perspiring amber. Grabbing the empty bottle, he carried it out to the front porch, where he unzipped his pants and peed into the bottle until it was full again. Groaning, he squinted his swollen eyes against the yellow light of the late September sun. He screwed the top back on the bottle, yawed back, and threw it far into the deep brush, beyond Burdy's property, where it struck a rock jutting up from the earth and broke into bits and shards. Then, Rain leaned over the tips of his boots edging the porch and puked violently.

It had been one hell of a night, ever since he opened that drawer in Burdy's house and found those letters postmarked from Bayeux, France. Rain hadn't read a single one of them. Not yet. He figured he would someday, probably, but it is one thing for a boy to grow up believing he was orphaned through the tragic deaths of his parents, and quite another to realize that what the boy in him believed

2

to be the truth had never been true. His father had not died a war hero. He wasn't dead at all. Zebulon Hurd had abandoned his family. He'd gone off willingly, under the guise of fighting for his country, nevermore to return.

As the rage of a boy abandoned rose up like the spirits of the evil departed, Rain hunkered over the edge of the porch and wretched again and again, heaving until there was nothing left, save for a bitter yellow bile that he swallowed back.

Chapter 2

The nurses at Knoxville's University of Tennessee Medical Center weren't a particularly religious or superstitious bunch. Whenever family members of the ailing came to visit and carried on about how God answered their prayers through this miracle or that one, the nurses would just nod their starched white caps in what appeared to be agreement. On those occasions when God faltered and someone died, and the bereaved consoled themselves with remarks about how God had called their loved ones home because he needed more angels, the nurses would retreat to the break room, rolling their eyes, shaking their heads.

"If any place needs more angels it's earth, not heaven." This was the common refrain of Thomasina Woodson, the night nurse supervisor. Woodson had relocated to Knoxville from Baltimore after leaving her sorry, no-count husband, a discourteous and mean-spirited man who abused her in every way except with his fists. Art Woodson took great pride in the fact that he never struck his wife, although it never gave him a moment's pause to demean and degrade her in every other way. He pleasured in the control he had over her.

Art was a family law attorney with a reputation for bribing judges and threatening younger, less-experienced lawyers. The smug attorney figured he was entitled to mistreating people. He was less handsome than he believed himself to be, but far more successful at making money than even he thought possible, all of which made it easy for Art to deceive others into thinking he was an upright citizen, a good father and a loving husband. Far from it. Art Woodson was a selfish excuse of a human being.

Art cheated on Thomasina from their wedding day forward. Of course, Thomasina didn't find out the truth of all that until years of marital misery had passed, and she finally grew so sick and tired of Art's hateful ways that she began to envision mixing anti-freeze into his brandy.

She had graciously dismissed Art's carelessness when he abandoned her on her thirtieth birthday. Instead of planning something special, Art took a trip to Mexico with his brother. Later, Thomasina had considered it bad luck when Art missed the birth of their second son. He was reportedly at a judicial convention in Nyack, New York. When Thomasina's water broke three weeks early, her sister, Eliza, had been unable to track Art down at the convention. By the time Art returned to Baltimore a week later, Thomasina was already at home with their newborn son.

Eliza, who had been at her sister's side the entire time, stayed on for a few days to help care for the boys. She never mentioned to Thomasina, not even after the divorce, how Art had snuck into her bed that second night. Eliza had woken to Art groping her up underneath her gown, but before she could scream, he'd clamped his hand down over her mouth and ordered her to remain quiet. "Don't scream! You'll frighten the boys."

Eliza kept quiet but put up a fierce struggle, biting Art on the fleshy part of his forearm so hard she drew blood. With his free hand, he slapped her upside the head, and she was forced to let go, otherwise she might have taken a chunk out of him. He left the room, furious, and insisted the next day that Eliza needed to go home. "Caring for our children is your job," he told Thomasina, " not your sister's!"

Thomasina didn't think it possible, but after the birth of their second child, Art grew even more controlling. In previous years, when Art was in law school, Thomasina had been the primary provider, working the swing shift at John Hopkins. Never did it occur to either one of them that the monies she brought home were hers and hers alone. Between her salary and Art's school loans, there were at least enough funds to pay the rent, buy the groceries, and even go out to an occasional movie or dinner. Thomasina had wanted to keep working after Art opened his law office and began to grow it into one of Baltimore's most successful practices, but Art demanded she quit, using her desire to start a family as the excuse. Art understood that as long as Thomasina wasn't earning her own monies, she was dependent on him for everything. He enjoyed that control immensely.

It wasn't long after the incident with Eliza that Art started treating Thomasina like she was his hired help. He paid her a "salary" and instructed her to use this meager allowance to pay for all the household needs, including groceries, which he meticulously kept track of.

Yes, earth definitely needed more angels than heaven did. And Thomasina knew that one of those angels was her best friend, Patti Jane. The two of them sat over coffee at Read's Drugstore as Thomasina detailed Art's offenses that finally led her to file for divorce after seventeen years of marriage. "One day, when the boys were about five and seven, he blew up over me buying a carton of orange juice." Thomasina shook her head as she stirred creamer into her steaming brew. "Can you imagine that? Orange juice? The boys loved orange juice, but after that incident, I never bought it again."

For her part, Patti Jane, a hairdresser, had noticed that divorced people possessed a need to talk through their losses the same way a surviving widow or widower might. Profound loss required hours of debriefing, it seemed. And Patti Jane was willing to listen. Even more, she felt that it was time to reveal something she'd never told her friend—that Art had assaulted her in the ladies' room during the couple's wedding reception.

"He raped you and you never told me, your very best friend since eighth grade?" Thomasina asked, her spoon frozen in the air above her mug.

6

"He didn't rape me," Patti Jane corrected. "I mean, he might have intended to, might have gotten away with it, if Graham hadn't heard my cries and come into that stall and yanked Art off of me."

Thomasina sighed. She'd been divorced from Art for two years, and yet there were still wrongs that she was learning about for the first time.

"Why didn't you come to me that night?" Thomasina implored. "How could you not warn me about the man I'd just married?" Her dark lashes were moist, her green eyes, usually flickering with joy, were clouded, troubled.

"This right here is why," Patti Jane replied, waving open palms before her girlfriend. "I knew how much it would hurt you. Art was drunk. It was your wedding. How could I tell you the man you had just married had sexually assaulted me? Art would have denied it, called me a liar. He never liked me when he was sober and you know it. Even before the wedding, he kept you isolated from everybody who loved you best. Be honest—would you have believed me if I had told you then?" Patti Jane wondered if she should have kept the secret forever. She grasped her nearly empty coffee cup and stared down into it, like a vagrant trying to draw warmth from the dying embers of a burn barrel.

"Probably not," Thomasina conceded. "Probably not." Reaching across the red dinette table, Thomasina wrapped her hands around Patti Jane's. "Listen, I'm sorry for what happened to you. Sorry I ever married Arthur Woodson. Can you ever forgive me?"

"Forgive you?" Patti Jane said. "Girl, Art is the one who ought to be apologizing. Not you. The only wrong thing you did was love the wrong man. He never understood how lucky he was to be loved by a woman as beautiful and kind as you. He always underestimated you and your powers."

"He did, didn't he?" Thomasina's ruby red lips parted as she flashed one of her brilliant smiles. The divorce had made her a wealthy woman. She took half of all that Art had amassed over the course of their marriage, including half of his retirement. It seemed Art wasn't the only meticulous note-taker in the household. Thomasina had gathered proof of his various investments and sources of income prior to filing for divorce. She was well prepared.

A few weeks after that conversation, Thomasina left Baltimore for Knoxville. Douglas, her youngest son, was enrolled at the University of Tennessee. The oldest boy, Terry, had moved off to Montana two years prior. As much as she didn't like to admit it, Thomasina had always been closer to Douglas. Terry was too much like his daddy, a restless soul who never cared much for anyone but himself.

Douglas was more than happy to have his mother follow him to Knoxville. He knew she would respect his boundaries, and he enjoyed the comfort of having her nearby where he could look out for her if she needed him.

Landing a job wasn't a problem for Thomasina. Hospitals were always in desperate need of nurses willing to take the swing shift, and she preferred that shift because it helped her avoid the lonely supper hour without a family to feed. She'd been working the swing shift in Knoxville for a little over a year when a gunshot victim by the name of Burdy Luttrell got transferred from ICU to a bed on the third floor, Thomasina's floor.

That Luttrell woman had Thomasina rethinking all her notions about heaven and hell and humanity on the whole. For the first time in her adult life, she was beginning to give credence to the things others had counted as superstitions and she had always counted as nonsense.

8

Chapter 3

"Momma?" Wheedin whispered as she leaned close to Burdy's face. "There's somebody here to see you."

"Tell them I ain't up to company," Burdy said, wiping drool from the corner of her mouth with the back of her hand. She had been dozing again. Damn blue pills. Damn Nurse Thomasina.

Thomasina was picking up a couple of extra shifts that week, working the day shift as well as the swing one, so she happened to be the one who insisted that Burdy take the pills morning, noon, and night. Burdy tried telling the nurse that she didn't need any pain pills, especially the kind that made her nearly comatose. Burdy had worked at Pressmen's Home long enough to know that medical personnel liked to keep their patients doped up, particularly those they considered "difficult," and she was certain that everybody within earshot of her room would label her that way.

She knew the other patients had overheard her and Wheedin arguing. They'd heard Burdy cuss Wheedin a blue streak after Wheedin suggested that her momma must be mistaken about taking some trip to France. Surely she was delirious and just needed more rest. That stirred something fierce in Burdy, and she let loose a string of words so profane that Mrs. Bettie Mae from the next room beat on the wall with her cane till Burdy shut up.

Wheedin was convinced that the incident at Laidlow's Pharmacy must have damaged more than Burdy's leg. She feared it may have destroyed her momma's memory, too. Wheedin had an appointment with Dr. Barnes to discuss the matter at 3:30, in an hour and a half, but right now Detective Wiley was waiting impatiently just outside Burdy's hospital room. He'd been sent by Chief Conley

9

and given firm orders to have a little chat with Burdy about whatever she could remember from the crime scene at Bean Station.

"I can't send him away, Momma. He's a lawman," Wheedin said.

"Of course you can," Burdy replied. "Just tell him I ain't up to company." She yanked a tissue from the box and patted the extra spit off her face. "Mash that button and raise this bed up."

Wheedin did as her momma told her. Then she straightened the pillows behind Burdy's back. Not an easy task for somebody with one arm, but Wheedin didn't permit herself to wallow over such things. She'd learned to make do with one arm long ago.

Burdy fiddled with the bedcovers, straightening them out as best she could while still tucked in.

Detective Wiley walked into the room, uninvited. "Sorry, Mrs. Luttrell, I don't mean to bother you…"

"Why sure you do," Burdy said. "You wouldn't be here otherwise."

Wiley grimaced. He hated hospitals. Always had, even as a little boy. His grandpa died in this very hospital when Wiley was ten. It was a freak accident, and decades later Wiley still hadn't gotten over the terror of it.

Grandpa Ginsey had been umping Wiley's ballgame. Wiley was inching off second base, thinking about stealing third, when the batter took a loose-grip swing and the bat came flying out of his hands, willy-nilly, and somehow struck Grandpa Ginsey just so and knocked him out cold. Some there that day who witnessed the whole thing up close swore it was an act of a Sovereign God. Wiley wasn't so sure himself.

"Glad to see you are feeling better, Mrs. Luttrell," Wiley said. He pulled a pen and a pad out of his jacket pocket.

"Whoever told you I was feeling better might as well pissed on your leg and told you it was raining," Burdy snapped. "I feel like a herd of wild boars have been feasting upon me after running me down in my own back forty."

"Yes, ma'am. I could see how you might feel that way. You are one lucky woman to have survived at all."

"That's what the doctor keeps saying, ain't it, Momma?" Wheedin chimed in.

"That doctor don't know shit from Shinola," Burdy remarked. "How many times I got to tell you? A person ain't lucky to survive a shooting. A lucky person is the one who never gets shot at to begin with. I would have been lucky if I'd been able to go into Laidlow's and buy that card for Leela like I planned without getting maimed. But I've had thousands of such lucky moments in my lifetime with nary a comment from anyone. Nobody ever stopped me in Rogersville or Surgoinsville to tell me how lucky I was to be able to walk about freely without being the target of the day for some lunatic." Her face reddened and kinks of white hair plonked out along her hairline. Burdy was sweatin' mad.

"You got a point there, Mrs. Luttrell," Wiley said, taking account of Burdy's agitated state. Wiley had hoped to diffuse any anxiety the old woman might have about speaking with him; instead, he'd unwittingly managed to escalate it.

"Momma, try not to get so worked up. Detective Wiley is just trying to do his job," Wheedin said. She wasn't the least bit shy about bossing her momma. She never had been. When she was younger, Burdy found Wheedin's spirited nature amusing, but not at this moment.

Burdy sized up Detective Wiley. He wasn't what you'd call easy on the eyes, but he was passable. His orange hair was faded and white around the temples. His cheeks had a natural peach tone, as if he had smeared on dime-store rouge before leaving the house. His hands were thick like those of a field hand, freckled on the back. She was sure that some women likely found the detective attractive, the sort of women who were prone to taking in strays dressed in

11

ready-to-wear. Burdy never had much use for a man lacking a good stiff crease. She used to spray Tibbis's shirts with water, roll them just so, and stick them in the freezer for a day or two before ironing them. Store-bought spray starch was inferior in every way to a good dousing of water mist and twelve hours in the freezer.

Detective Wiley probably didn't know practical things like that, Burdy reasoned. It had been her lifelong experience that men who worked in law enforcement gave little thought to how they dressed. They had so many other details to attend to—shell casings, blood splatters, liars, and such. To his credit, Wiley seemed a patient man, willing to wait until he was spoken to before speaking. Burdy had half a mind to keep him waiting for a good long while, if only she had the energy for it.

"I won't take up much of your time, Mrs. Luttrell," Wiley said.

Burdy stared burn holes into the detective. Her way of letting him know she knew better than that. "Spit out your questions fast, then," she said. "Who knows how much time I got left?"

Detective Wiley chuckled. Nothing wrong with the old woman's mind, that was for dang sure. "Can you tell me what you remember from that day prior to the shooting?"

Burdy told the detective how she had coaxed Mayne into taking her up to Lincoln Memorial University for a class on healing roots, only to find out that she knew more than the person teaching the class. So they left and went over to The Gap House in Cumberland and had lunch. Then, on their return trip home, they'd stopped at Laidlow's in Bean Station.

"We was just going to stop in for a minute," Burdy said. "I was going to pick up a card for a friend and Mayne needed something to settle her stomach. The chili she ate hadn't set well with her."

Detective Wiley took notes as Burdy talked. He knew that most of what he was writing wouldn't be helpful, but he also knew that when it came to details, the smallest one could often prove most crucial.

"I don't remember much else after that," Burdy said, a note of finality in her voice.

"You don't remember going into the store?" Wiley asked.

"Not really."

"You don't recall the sales clerk who waited on you?"

"I don't. I don't even know if I spoke to a sales clerk or not," Burdy said.

"What is the very last thing you remember?"

Wheedin watched as her momma studied the crisscrossing lines in her palms, as if somewhere in those deep crevasses resided memories yet undiscovered. Quietly, she whispered to the detective, "Momma's had some problems with her memory since the shooting."

Wiley nodded, signaling that he understood. "It's okay, Mrs. Luttrell."

Burdy rubbed her hands together, then ran them across her cheeks. The empty IV bag hanging beside her bed beeped. "Isn't it odd that a person can remember what happened forty years ago but can't recall what happened last week on one of the most troubling days of their lives?"

"That's not so surprising," Wiley said. "Trauma affects people differently. Don't let it be a worriment. I'm sure some of it will come back to you soon enough." He closed his notebook and returned it and his pen to his coat pocket. "I've got other people that I need to talk to still. I'll get with you again. Maybe after you go home?"

Burdy didn't respond one way or another. Trouble brewed in her aqua eyes like a late afternoon storm threatening Gulf waters. She looked to be in some far-off place.

Wheedin pulled at the corners of the bedspread, smoothing it out.

"Thank you," Wiley said. He headed for the door, and Wheedin followed. In the hallway, he asked, "When do you think your momma might be headed home?"

"I'm not sure. Doctor hasn't said yet. If it were up to Momma she'd go this afternoon. They got the infection under control and the wound is beginning to heal, thank the good Lord, but Momma hasn't been right in the head since all this happened." Wheedin whispered that last bit, fearing Burdy might hear her. Burdy might not be right in the head, but there was nothing wrong with her hearing. Tibbis used to say that if a tree fell anywhere on Horseshoe Ridge, Burdy could be uptown and still hear it.

"What do you mean by that?" Wiley asked.

"I don't know exactly," Wheedin replied. "Ever since she woke up, Momma's been talking about things that never happened."

"What kind of things?" Wiley watched as a white-clad orderly pushed a portable potty wheelchair from the room across the hall. Wiley hoped that, when he died, it wouldn't be in a place that smelled of Lysol and piss. *Please God, let me die on the banks of the Holston with a string of fish in my hand and a gun on my hip.*

"Nonsense, really," Wheedin said. She rubbed the scarred place where her arm used to be. That's the thing nobody ever warned her about, how somebody who's lost a limb never quits feeling the pain of having it gone. Sometimes Wheedin would reach for things with an arm that wasn't there, her mind stubbornly refusing to acknowledge the absent limb. She made do with one arm, but she never quit missing the other one. "She keeps talking about someone named Clint and about her trips to France."

"This Clint fellow, could he be a neighbor of hers, a coworker?"

"I suppose." Wheedin frowned. "A lot of new people have moved into the Bend since I left. And I haven't kept track of everyone she's helped heal over the years, but Momma's never been to France. Far as I know she's never been further north than Abingdon, Virginia. Well, except she did go to Colorado once to visit some cousin, but that was years ago. I don't know how all this talk of France came about."

"What does the doctor say about it?"

"Dr. Barnes said she could have some medically induced amnesia. He said sometimes when a person goes under anesthesia, it messes with their memory center. For that first week or so, I wasn't even sure if Momma knew who she was. I'm supposed to meet with the doctor about it in a bit."

As he left the hospital, Wiley reflected that it was just like he always suspected: there's nothing like a hospital to make the well sick, the walking lame, and the living dead.

Chapter 4

The shooting at Bean Station was all anybody was talking about. The shooter was still on the loose, and for the first time in anyone's memory, people in the Bend took to locking their doors. Con Christian went around stomping on people's porches and hollering over fence posts about the destruction surely coming: "I looked, and behold, an ashen horse, and he who sat on it had the name Death, and Hades was following with him. Authority was given to them over a fourth of the earth, to kill with the sword and with famine and with pestilence and by the wild beasts of the earth."

People in the Bend usually took Con in stride, but these weren't usual times. Con's carrying on got on people's nerves. Watson Loxley, the nephew of the fellow who worked on Ida Mosely's sister's place, was one of the ones killed. Most of the people in the Bend knew Ida, knew her sister, and even if they didn't know Watson, they might as well have for all the fear the shooting put in them.

"Executed him," Ida said. "Shot that poor boy in the back of the head like he was a communist spy or a dog needing put down."

Watson Loxley had dropped out of high school and gone to work as a farmhand because he couldn't work with his brain. He'd never learned to read. Some blamed his momma, said she had gone to a funeral when she was no more than three months pregnant, which was pretty much an open invitation for bad spirits to harm the unborn. Watson wanted to read in the worst way, but his mind couldn't un-jumble the letters and form them into words. So, while the other kids at Grainger Elementary were reading *The Bridge to Terabithia*, Watson was flipping through Ranger Rick magazines, looking at all the pictures and guessing at the puzzles. He never went past the sixth grade.

Only nineteen, Watson was the youngest person killed at Laidlow's. The others slain were a married couple, Hunk and Mary Nelle Kincer, who owned and ran the pharmacy. They had bought it from Dukey and Pat Laidlow just three years prior. It was reported that Hunk, a former lineman for UT, had covered his wife of thirty-seven years with his own body after the gunman ordered them to lie facedown on the nasty concrete floor. Not that it mattered, given that the gunman shot them all execution-style—all, that is, except for Burdy. For some inexplicable reason, he didn't shoot to kill Burdy, just to maim her.

"Was he hoping to make her suffer, or was that his lopsided idea of mercy?" Wiley wondered aloud. He gave the turnip greens on his plate a good dousing of vinegar and looked up at Chief Conley. The chief was sitting across the yellow dinette table at Minnie's Diner, shoveling a forkful of macaroni and cheese into his mouth.

"Who can know what makes a crazed person do what they do," Conley replied, his cheek still full. "That's why come we call them crazy."

"I reckon so," Wiley mused.

"We get anything back on those plates Miss Bernadette thinks she saw?" Conley took a gulp of sweet tea. Wiley didn't know how his boss could drink that stuff. Minnie's tea was so sweet it made his teeth ache.

"Naw. Not yet," Wiley answered, then started as a young woman two tables over dropped her knife and fork on the floor. Man, was he jumpy. "I did get over to Knoxville to see the Widow Luttrell."

"How was that?"

"Hardly worth the drive. Her daughter is going to let me know when she's back home. Not sure she's going to be much help to us, though. Guess she's been having some problems remembering."

17

"Understandable, given all she's been through," Conley said. "She's old as dirt, ain't she?"

"I dunno," Wiley said. "She don't look any older than Minnie over there." Wiley nodded towards the stout woman serving up mac and cheese.

"Report said she's eighty."

"I'd never have thunk it." Wiley stood up to clear their empty plates and wadded-up napkins from the table. He dropped the napkins in the trash and placed the plates in the washing bin. The chief was standing next to the door, waiting on Wiley when Clive Conley walked in.

Wiley had no use for his boss's son. Clive was a bad seed, stubborn as a mule and not nearly as smart. He liked to spend other people's money, drink other people's beer, and sleep in other people's beds. Clive went through girlfriends haphazardly, like a GI on a ten-day pass to Bangkok. His last one, Sudie Boone, didn't take kindly to Clive's rambling ways. When she found out Clive was stepping out on her, she liked to run him flat over on Main Street in the middle of the day. He ended up in the hospital with a fractured hip, which put at least a temporary end to his catting around.

"I'll see you back at the office," Wiley said, brushing past his boss, not even bothering to give Clive a nod of recognition.

"Sure thing," Conley replied. "I'll be there directly."

Chapter 5

Leela's birthday came and went without much fanfare. The quilting guild had planned a potluck gathering at the Bend's community center, but when Burdy ended up in the hospital everything was postponed. Nobody had the heart for celebrating after the shooting.

Unwilling to let Leela's eightieth birthday pass without any fanfare, however, Doc reheated some pinto beans and fried up some potato cakes from leftover mashed potatoes. He seasoned the cakes with a pinch of salt and a heavy dousing of black pepper, which Doc figured could make near about anything taste better. Leela was all the time accusing Doc of being part Cajun because he liked to pepper whatever he was eating.

Doc picked some black-eyed Susans from the yard and stuck them in a small purple vase that had belonged to Leela's momma long ago. He wiped down the plastic covering Leela kept on the table to protect the varnished wood and set the flowers in the middle, then pulled out the Blue Willow dishes that had been Maizee's and Zeb's and set the table for three, just in case.

But neither he nor Leela had heard from Rain since they'd brought him home from Knoxville four days ago. Rain had left the house on Sunday, saying he had to go see a man about a horse. Doc and Leela knew good and well that he was headed off to Burdy's house and to the rental out back that Rain once knew as home. Leela tried to get Doc to go over Monday and check on him, but Doc protested.

"Rain's a grown man. He don't need looking after no more."

"Don't you think it quare that we ain't heard a word from him since he went over there?" Leela argued.

"No," Doc said. "It's probably good for him to have the place to himself without Burdy or us peering in on him. He may have even hiked up to Horseshoe Falls and spent a few nights camping underneath God's big sky. I know if I lived in a busy city like him, I'd head to the hills every chance I got. Sometimes silence is the thing a man needs most." Doc cut his eyes at Leela in a telling way.

Leela didn't argue no more after that. She kept her worries to herself, but on Tuesday afternoon she'd walked over to Burdy's place, hoping to run into Rain.

Peering into the windows of Maizee and Zeb's old place, she could tell he'd been there. The linens on the bed were rumpled, like he'd slept on top of the covers. The old percolating coffee pot was on the cold burner, and a coffee cup waited on the counter. It wouldn't do her much good to knock or call out Rain's name, so she spent the afternoon yanking weeds out of the flower beds around Burdy's place. She swept the back porch and dusted the rockers. When it got near on the gloaming hour, Leela headed back home. Maybe Doc was right. Maybe Rain was finding solace in the hills after all.

And then he showed up for Leela's birthday dinner, just as Doc fished the potato cakes from the frying pan. He came into the kitchen through the back door, went straight to the sink and washed his hands. It looked like a raccoon had slept atop his head, his dark hair, still as thick as when he was a young boy, poking out every which way. His clothes and any exposed skin were crusted with dirt. He resembled a miner but looked more like he was powdered in brown cocoa than black coal.

"Lord God Almighty, where have you been, son?" Doc exclaimed. He set the plate of hot potato cakes on the table.

Rain, still scrubbing his hands, had his back turned toward Doc, so he didn't hear the question until he turned around and Doc repeated it so Rain could read his uncle's lips.

"Spent a couple of nights up at Horseshoe Falls," Rain replied.

"Were the skeeters bad?" Leela asked. "They can be awfully bad this time year, especially near those pools of water. Why, last time I was up there, gosh, it must've been back in '83 or '84, they near about eat me alive."

"Have a seat, birthday girl," Doc said, pulling out a chair for his bride.

"You shouldn't have made such a fuss," Leela said. "I'd just as soon forget what an old woman I've become. But thank you very much."

"You don't look a day over sixty to me," Rain said. "And nope, no mosquito bites, but then again, I'm not as sweet as you, not nearly as appealing." He winked at Leela.

They steered clear of any troubling matters throughout the meal, partly because they were all trying hard to celebrate, and partly because neither Doc nor Leela knew how to broach hard things. They both took the position that if Rain had something that needed saying, he'd say it.

After supper, Doc cut Leela a slice of the apple pie he'd bought at Donnie's Market and put a dollop of Blue Bell ice cream on top of it. He stuck one red candle in the middle of the ice cream, lit it, and then he and Rain sang Happy Birthday to Leela.

Rain ate every bit of his piece of store-bought apple pie and helped himself to another scoop of ice cream without divulging a single word about the box of letters he'd found in the bottom of Burdy's dresser drawer. He didn't tell Leela or Doc that he had hidden the box in his mother's hope chest. He had yet to read them.

"Any word on when Burdy might be coming home?" Rain asked. He was hoping to avoid her for a while.

"I called up to the hospital yesterday," Leela said. "Wheedin said she hoped to bring her home tomorrow. The quilting circle is getting meals together, and I suspect some of us will be helping out for the time being. Wheedin has to get on back to South Carolina."

Leela stood up and began clearing the dishes, but Doc stopped her. "None of that, young lady. It's your birthday. I'll warsh these up soon as you open that gift I brung you." Doc put a tiny box in the place where Leela's dish had been. It was wrapped in a pink floral paper and tied off with a pale pink bow. Leela knew it was a jewelry box before she ever saw the little gold sticker that read "Hoover's Jeweler: Kingsport's Finest Since 1886."

Leela opened the card first. Every year on her birthday, Doc wrote Leela a poem. His was the only poetry Leela enjoyed, other than the poetry of the Bible, of course.

Who am I apart from you?
Our bodies have become as one.
To love, did I first have to be loved?
Your spirit, graceful, embraces all
Without hesitation. You love, wholeheartedly,
And I am the better man for it.
You are the heart of my world.

Doc reached over and wiped a tear from Leela's cheek with his thumb. Rain knew he should look away, give Doc and Leela this moment, but he couldn't help watching them. The tenderness of their appreciation for one another was mesmerizing, even after all these years and all the heartaches they'd suffered. Rain couldn't help but wish he had someone to share that kind of love with him.

Leela untied the ribbon and unwrapped the box. Inside was a ring with four multi-colored stones: a ruby, a sapphire, an emerald, and a peridot.

"Oh, my gracious! It is beautiful!" Leela declared, slipping the ring on. "Fits perfectly, too."

"Mr. Hoover said it's the latest thing," Doc said proudly. He was grinning. "They call it a mother's ring. See? There's a stone for each of our birthdays. Rain's and Maizee's, too."

The barren part of Leela could not hold back. With her hands covering her face, she hunched over her lap and wept full throttle. Doc patted her shaking shoulders. "There, there," he said.

Rain pulled a hanky from his pocket and handed it to Leela. She wiped her eyes, blew her nose.

"You can keep it now," Rain said and they all laughed. Leela stuffed it into her apron pocket. "I'm sorry I didn't get you a gift from one of those fancy stores up in Kingsport, but I did bring you a little something." Rain placed a brown paper poke on the table. "It's just a little something I made up at Horseshoe Falls."

Leela reached into the sack and pulled out an intricately carved angel whose wingspan was about the size of Doc's wide-open hand.

"You carved this?" Leela asked, clasping the angel right up next to her heart.

Rain nodded.

"I didn't know you knew how to whittle," Doc said.

"All those years of watching you paid off, I guess," Rain replied.

Doc took the angel from Leela and turned it over and over again, as if inspecting it for flaws. "You done good, son. It's one of the finest pieces of carved wood I've ever seen."

"Made it from a branch that fell off the old grandfather chestnut. It's dying, you know. That old grandfather chestnut."

"I heard that," Doc said. "Con Christian says the grandfather chestnut dying is a sign of the end times."

"Con Christian says every thunderclap is a sign of the end times," Leela interjected.

"That's true," Doc conceded. "But that tree managed to survive the blight when every other chestnut in these parts died from it. The way I figure it, that tree has borne witness to every single hardship to hit these mountains."

"And it's woken to every single sunrise, too, I bet," Leela countered.

"I suppose so," Doc said. "Wonder how come it's dying now."

"Worn out, I imagine," Rain said. "I can't say I blame it. Sooner or later, a living thing tires of living."

Doc looked over at Leela, worry in his eyes. Leela exchanged the same concerned look. Was Rain trying to tell them something? Had his mama's illness settled over him all these years later? Had Rain grown weary with living? Had he come across something at Burdy's that upset him?

Chapter 6

Burdy had her bags packed by 8 a.m. She told everybody who was anybody that she was going home that day, including Loretta, the candy striper Burdy never willingly engaged in conversation because the girl talked so much and so fast it made a person liable to keel over from dizziness. Nurse Thomasina had dropped by that morning before her shift ended to go over some instructions with Wheedin.

"The doctor is going to release your momma today. When he does, remember she's going to need twenty-four-hour care at least for the next week. Keep the bandages clean, and change them out every day. Here," Thomasina picked up a paper poke. "I packed some extra gauze and tape for you. There's also some antibacterial cream in there that I want you to apply three times a day."

Trying to ignore them, Burdy stood before the bathroom mirror braiding her hair. Once home, she had to find a way to get shed of Wheedin for a bit so she could call Clint. They had a ritual of talking by phone every Saturday and Wednesday. Two weeks had passed since she last spoke to him, and Burdy knew he'd be sick with worry. She wouldn't be the least bit surprised if he showed up on her doorstep any day now. Clint was all the time chiding Burdy about how busy she kept herself. He had long thought that she ought to pack up and move to France, let him take care of her. Burdy was tempted mightily, but she could never figure out how to explain things to people in the Bend, to Doc, Leela-Ma, Rain, and, of course, Wheedin, who would never excuse her momma an affair with a Frenchman, of all people!

Burdy had never told anyone about meeting up with Zeb all those years ago, or about the letters they'd exchanged, or about her love affair with Clint. She couldn't figure out how a person is supposed to go about announcing such things. It seemed entirely inappropriate to just blurt it out during Wednesday evening prayer service the way some people were prone to do. Why, just last month, Maybelle Lou Dean had stood before the congregation and announced that her husband had contracted a sexually transmitted disease from having extra-marital relations with Daisy Goforth, a hairdresser from up at Johnson City. Talk about your revelations.

Burdy figured Pastor would hurry on past Maybelle's request for prayer, but no, he called Maybelle to the front of the church and interviewed her right there on the spot. Before God and most of the Bend, Pastor Jason asked her the details of how her husband, Brother Ben, had got caught up in such sin. Burdy figured most of what transpired was owing to Pastor Jason's lack of experience. He was an outsider, come to the Bend from one of them fancy New York City seminaries, although he himself grew up in New Jersey. He didn't fit in at all, but everybody in the Bend was too nice to tell him just yet. They'd tolerate Yankees for about a year. After that, most hoped he'd come to realize he'd worn out his welcome, and nobody would have to feel bad about telling Pastor Jason God was calling him elsewhere.

"Momma? Momma?" Wheedin called out.

"I'll be there directly," Burdy called back. "Just tying off my hair." Burdy wrapped an elastic band around the end of her long, thick braid. Burdy's hair had turned white as egret feathers. She didn't mind; she was happy to swap out a bit of vainglory for a bit of common respect. She knew women with white hair are afforded more respect than those with black hair. Now if she could only get Wheedin to stop treating her like a child.

Burdy hobbled out of the bathroom with the aid of a walker. "Here I be!" she announced. "You looking for me?"

"I thought you might want to say good-bye to Nurse Woodson before she leaves," Wheedin said. "She's been so helpful to us."

"Nurse Woodson?" Burdy asked. "You mean Thomasina?"

"Yes," Wheedin replied.

Burdy knew she shouldn't, but she couldn't help but be delighted whenever she was able to put Wheedin on edge. It was Burdy's way of reminding her daughter that she was the daughter.

"Hold on a second, Thomasina," Burdy said. "I have a little something for you."

Thomasina waved her off. "We aren't allowed to accept gifts from patients. Seeing you upright is all the gift I need."

"Hogwash!" Burdy said. "I'll give you a gift if I darn well please. Who's going to stop me?" And with that, Burdy pulled a hanky from her purse and passed it to Thomasina. "Be careful when you unfold it," she said.

Thomasina cupped her hands underneath the embroidered handkerchief and carefully unwrapped it. Inside was a glass ball the size of her palm, pink and lavender like a summer sunset.

"Hold it up to the light," Burdy said. "I put some of my hair inside it. See?"

Thomasina did as she was instructed, and, yes, she could see strands of hair balled up inside the glass.

"It's a witching ball," Burdy explained. "The hair helps catch the evil spirits and keep them away. And honey, I figure you can use all the help you can get keeping that jackass of an ex-husband away."

"Momma!" Wheedin declared. "That's so rude!"

"No, no," Thomasina said, laughing. "Your momma is right. My ex is a jackass, and if a wad of hair inside a ball will help keep him away, I'm going to hang one in every room of the house. Thank you." She hugged Burdy gently.

They had grown close, the two of them. Thomasina didn't usually get to know her patients as well as she'd come to know Burdy. She certainly had never shared with another patient the stories she'd shared with Burdy. Most of her patients slept during the evening shift, but the gunshot victim was almost always awake. It was as if Burdy didn't need sleep once she woke from that weeklong coma and was transferred out of ICU. She stayed in a regular room on Thomasina's floor for nearly two weeks.

Typically patients only spent a couple of nights on the third floor, so two weeks stretched into what seemed like a year. Thomasina found herself making up excuses to check on her new-found friend so they could swap stories. If a person could cast a truth spell on another, Burdy had done that to the good nurse. On the very first night, Thomasina had divulged the details of her un-happy marriage during the midnight check.

She'd found Burdy sitting up in bed, scribbling a note, when she stopped in to change out an IV. Thomasina turned the alarm button off. Checked the IV bag. Declared to no one in particular the bag needed changing and proceeded to change it out. Burdy was preoccupied writing, so Thomasina tried her level best not to disrupt her any more than was necessary. It was Burdy who spoke first.

"You look just like that actress I seen on the television last night." She pointed at the TV hanging from the corner.

"Which actress is that?" Thomasina asked. "Elizabeth Taylor?" She winked at Burdy as she took her hand.

"I don't know her name," Burdy said. "I don't watch TV at home, but there really isn't much else to do here while a person lays around trying to heal up."

"So it wasn't Elizabeth Taylor?" Thomasina fooled with the drip line.

"She's a spit of a woman, like you," Burdy said. "The movie was called Norma Rae. It was pretty good. Have you seen it?" She put her pen down.

"Isn't that the one where Sally Field climbs atop a counter in the textile mill and holds up a union sign?"

"Yes," Burdy said, nodding her head. "What'd you say that actress's name is again?"

"Sally Field. I think she won an Oscar for that role," Thomasina said. "Do you mind if I take a look at your leg while I'm here?"

"No, go ahead," Burdy said, throwing back the covers. "I don't know nothing about any Oscars, but I liked that Norma Rae's fiery spirit, the way she fought for those people in that mill. I like a woman who has some spunk to her."

"Like you, you mean?" Thomasina said, smiling. The day shift nurses considered Mrs. Luttrell a difficult patient. There's no pleasing the old woman in Room 315, a daytime nurse had written on the chart.

"Yes, like me," Burdy replied. "But you do favor that Norma Rae woman."

"You mean Sally Field," Thomasina said.

"Whatever her name is. Hasn't anybody else ever told you that?"

"From time to time, somebody will mention it." Thomasina pulled the covers back up over Burdy and glanced at the empty recliner. "Was that your daughter whose been staying with you?" It was hard to forget the one-armed woman who had been at Burdy's side most every moment.

"Yes, but she got a hotel room tonight. Said she needed a shower and a good night's sleep."

"I bet."

"She's bossy but it's lonely without her," Burdy said. "Would you mind getting me some fresh water?" Burdy didn't plan on drinking a lot of water in the middle of the night, but she was looking for a reason to keep Thomasina around.

Thomasina got Burdy the water she requested and spent the next forty-five minutes talking with her about how she ended up moving from Baltimore, a story that, up until that night, Thomasina had told no one in Knoxville.

While Thomasina was happy that Burdy was on her feet, eager to get home, she was also sad to say good-bye. "I'm going to miss our late-night chats."

"Me, too," Burdy said. "Usually if I'm up talking at midnight it's to myself." She flashed a bright smile at Thomasina and at Wheedin, who didn't even notice as she was busy wiping down the bedside table and tidying up after her momma.

"Just leave it," Thomasina said. "Don't bother. The orderlies will clean it once you're gone."

"When do you think that will be?" Wheedin asked.

"I shouldn't think too awfully long," Thomasina said. "The doctor will be making his rounds in the next hour. Things will move pretty quickly after that, as they need these beds. Once he signs off, you'll get some last-minute instructions and then you can be on your way."

"Would you mind staying with Momma while I carry some of her things down to the car?" Wheedin asked.

"Not at all," Thomasina said. "But don't you want to wait until someone can help you?" Thomasina didn't want to state the obvious: How much stuff could a one-armed woman carry in a single trip?

"Thank you, but I've got it." Wheedin said, hoisting one bag across her armless side and picking up a suitcase with her good hand.

Burdy pushed her walker over to the edge of the bed and sat down. "That girl of mine," she said after Wheedin left, "she's as mule-headed as they come. She's always been an independent soul—I raised her that way on purpose—but since she lost that arm of hers, she's even more determined to do everything herself."

"How did she lose her arm?"

"She wasn't as lucky as you," Burdy replied. "She and her fella at the time got into it one day over something or another, and she ended up on the wrong side of a rifle. 'Course, she tells everybody it was an accident. Isn't that what every woman whose been abused tells people?"

"I suppose," Thomasina said. She leaned on the back of the recliner. Her feet were killing her after a long night shift. She couldn't wait to get home and take off the white support hose pinching her toes.

"It weren't long after that Wheedin up and moved off to South Carolina. She hardly ever comes back to the Bend and, far as I know, hasn't ever been with any other man."

"Really?" Thomasina was surprised. "But she's so beautiful. I would think she could have her pick."

"She could, but I reckon she ain't interested. Leastways if she is, she ain't never said."

Jane Pauley's voice floated down the hallway as somebody switched on The Today Show. Somebody in the next room flushed the toilet. A well-dressed man walked into the room across the hall carrying a cup of freshly brewed coffee.

"What about you?" Burdy asked.

"What about me?"

"You going to give love another go?"

"I don't know," Thomasina replied. "Much as I might like the idea that my one true love is out there somewhere, I am highly skeptical. Besides, I'm forty-three. Who's going to want an old woman like me?"

"Oh, you might be surprised," Burdy said. "I know I was."

"What surprised you, Momma?" Wheedin asked. She'd walked into the room on the tail-end of the conversation.

"People like you sneaking up on me," Burdy snapped. She was discombobulated by Wheedin's quick return and more than a bit flustered that her daughter had almost caught her divulging details of her relationship with Clint.

"Well, I should be going," Thomasina said, clearly uncomfortable. "Follow the doctor's orders and you won't have to see me anymore."

"Much as I'd like to avoid this hospital, I will miss you," Burdy said. "Be kind to yourself and don't let your heart harden. It ain't healthy."

Thomasina left the room quickly, waving behind her head. She didn't wipe away the tears until she was well past Burdy's room.

Chapter 7

The day after Leela's birthday dinner, Rain notified Ellis, his boss at Salve Regina College in Rhode Island that he would not be returning. Ellis urged him not to quit outright. Rain had spent the bulk of his career in Newport overseeing the school's admission programs. He was well respected throughout Rhode Island for his work as an advocate for disabled students. Under his leadership, Salve Regina had become a model of how to serve students with special needs. Rain was proud of the work he had accomplished, but for the first time since he was a young boy he did not want to leave the Bend. He craved the isolation and the silence the mountains offered.

Rain didn't tell Ellis that he didn't trust himself to be around people right now. Ever since he'd learned of his father's letters, the only emotion he felt was rage. It was as if his blood had turned to kerosene and he'd swallowed a fiery torch; he was burnt up from the inside out. The intensity of his own anger frightened him. It was Ellis who suggested that Rain should take a six-month leave for now and they'd reassess again in the spring. It was the worst possible time for such an agreement, given that the 1987–88 school year was just getting underway, but Rain agreed to the plan. At least this way he wouldn't have to figure out what to do with his house. He had some time to deal with all that. What he didn't know was what to do about Burdy once she got home.

Rain felt most betrayed by Burdy. Like a lot of people, he had long considered her one of the wisest people in the Bend. What in God's name had she been thinking? Why would she keep those letters from him all these years? Here she had been going around acting all high and mighty, like she was the truth-teller of the mountain, and the entire time she was lying through her eyeteeth to Rain and everybody else. What a crock of dookey. Rain resolved to avoid Burdy as best he could. It wouldn't be easy given he was staying at the house on her property, the one his parents had rented.

Leela was put out with Rain on account of his staying over at Burdy Luttrell's. She wanted him to stay with her and Doc, in his old bedroom, still decorated with the artifacts from his youth—his baseball glove signed by Babe Ruth, a Boston Red Sox baseball cap, frayed at the bill from all the times he yanked on it, and his collection of Sandy Koufax cards stuck around the dresser mirror. As a young boy, Rain liked that Sandy was a leftie like him.

Rain had forgotten how much he'd loved baseball as a boy. Doc had a friend, Harve Bass, who played for the Rogersville farm team. Doc and Rain used to catch the ferry across the Holston and go downriver to watch them play. Rain would sit beside Doc on hard bleachers during the sweatiest part of a hot Saturday, sharing a bag of boiled peanuts with him, and imagining himself playing for the major leagues one day. That was back before Rain went off to Knoxville and got so busy growing up he lost sight of the things he loved most—things like baseball and spending a Saturday afternoon sitting beside Doc. Rain couldn't remember the last time he'd watched a game, much less played in one. In college, he had gotten into running. It wasn't exactly a team sport like baseball, but Rain liked that he could fit running into his own schedule.

After he got off the phone with Ellis, Rain thought maybe a run would do him some good. It might ease the burning in his gut better than another night of drinking. He changed into a pair of blue shorts and a worn-out tee, strapped on his running shoes, and did a few stretches before heading out the gravel drive beside Burdy's house, past Con Christian's place, down the hill around the old grist mill, over the bridge that stretched across shattered earth where a creek would flow with enough rain, but there never was enough by summer's end. Rain ran past the barn falling in on itself at Dyke's corner, and just a ways beyond that, he eyed a flock of

34

wild turkeys strolling across a grassy field. Rain thought they looked like a bunch of Amish men searching for a good place to sneak a smoke. He didn't stop running until he reached McPheeter's place and saw Creed McPheeter outside working the tobacco.

Creed had his arms full of lugs, the tobacco leaves he'd yanked from the bottom of the plants. He dropped his load into a wheelbarrow at the end of the row and waved to Rain. Creed's daddy and Rain's daddy had been classmates at Rogersville Grade School when they were youngsters. Boog McPheeters tried to enter the Army when Zeb did, but they wouldn't have him. Said his heart wasn't strong enough, even though Boog was the same age as Zeb—leastways that's the story people at the Bend always retold whenever anyone brought Boog's name up, which wasn't often, on account of respect. Everybody knew how badly Boog felt about not being able to serve when all his classmates had gone off to fight.

After Zeb went missing and Maizee took her life, Boog constructed three crosses—one thirty feet tall, one twenty feet, and one fifteen feet—and stuck them on the highest hill he owned. Anywhere a person stood in Goshen Valley, they could look up east and see the tallest of those crosses. Boog had even rigged up lights that shone on the crosses year-round, from dusk to dawn. He never mentioned Zeb to nobody, but everyone knew that building those crosses was Boog's way of grieving what had come to pass. It was his personal memorial to the classmate he'd played dodge ball and stick ball with when they were both young'uns.

Looking beyond Creed and the rows of big-leafed tobacco to the hill with the crosses, Rain wondered what Boog would think now if he knew the truth about Zeb. Would he be angry, too?

"I thought maybe your daddy had gone and hired a girl to harvest his tobacco," Rain said. Creed shoved a handful of wavy, thick hair off his forehead. Sun-bleached, his golden locks fell to his shoulders.

"Piss on you," Creed replied. "You're just jealous." Creed stuck out his hand and Rain shook it.

"Probably right," Rain said. He turned away and spit before adding, "How could I help but not be jealous of a pretty boy like you?"

Creed had to listen carefully to make out what Rain was saying; his speech wasn't like that of most people. It wasn't hard to make out once a person got adjusted to the pattern, which had a nasal quality and an irregular spacing, but a fellow had to pay attention and listen better than usual. Sometimes if Rain said something he couldn't make out, Creed would take a wild guess and fill in the missing words. He was usually right.

"What can I say?" Creed smiled broadly, brightly. "Obviously, God loved me best."

"Well, there's all the proof we need to know that God is a woman after all. She's in love with you."

"Yeah, yeah. Who's chasing you, anyway? Somebody's husband?"

"Nobody. Just out getting some exercise."

"Good gawd, Rain. Don't nobody around here run unless somebody's after them. You want some exercise, grab that," Creed nodded toward the wheelbarrow. "I got to get this tobacco up to the barn." Rain grabbed the handles and followed Creed, who had picked up another armful of leaves from the end of a row.

The barn sat on an incline behind the white clapboard farmhouse. It was badly weathered, but inside, where the shadows fell cool across the dirt floor, the structure stood steady as the day it was first built. The sweet scent of tobacco and sunshine filled the barn. The rafters were already half-full of tobacco crinkling and yellowing. Creed handed Rain a ball of twine and the two began tying piles of the leaves together.

"The last time I did this job I was working alongside Kade Mashburn," Rain said. "We were young boys with big dreams."

"Kade Mashburn? I haven't seen him in a coon's age. Whatever happened to him? Last I heard he was living in Nashville."

Rain reached for Creed's pocketknife and cut a length of twine as long as his forearm. "He moved to Knoxville some years back. He's working for the DEA. Or leastways that's what he was doing last time I asked Wheedin Luttrell about him."

"No shit. The DEA?" Creed pulled a doobie from his shirt pocket, struck a match on the side of a stick, and lit the joint. After taking a drag, he passed it to Rain.

"No, thanks," Rain said, waving it off.

"Suit yourself." Creed took another hit. "What are you doing back in these parts? I thought you had up and moved off to Yankeeland."

"I did. Came back on account of that shooting over at Bean Station." Rain tied off another bunch of leaves.

"Yeah, that was some kind of sorry mess." Creed's tone was flat, like somebody who was reading the warnings off the side of a pill bottle, just reciting information. "Daddy said one of them shot was Burdy Luttrell."

"Yep."

"Is she how come you come back?" Creed took one last inhale, then pinched the tip end of the joint and stuck the remainder back in his shirt pocket. He heaved a bunch of the tied-off tobacco onto his shoulder and climbed the ladder to the rafters, where he proceeded to hang the bundles across a wire line for drying.

"Yes," Rain called up after him. "Burdy's the reason I come home."

"Well, you two were always tight as ticks on a hound. I never understood why you'd hang around with that old woman. She's got witching powers, you know. Daddy said her kin were the ones responsible for the haints in the Sensabaugh Tunnel."

Rain had long forgotten the stories about the watery old tunnel off Big Elm Road. The only locals who would pass through it belonged to that Belcher clan that lived on the far side of the tunnel. There wasn't a preacher or a lawman in all of Hawkins or Sullivan County that would call on the Belchers. Far as Rain knew, Burdy was the only soul who'd called on the family when their boy, Virgie, fell headlong into the well and drowned himself to death.

There wasn't but a few feet of water in that well. If Virgie had been nine or ten, he might have caught himself, might have survived the fall, but he was only six and had struck his head on the way down. It was a tragedy made all the worse because Virgie had been in the well all day and half the evening before Mr. Belcher come to realize what had happened to his boy. Mrs. Belcher sent for Burdy, and she went up to their place and prepared Virgie's body for burial, then conducted the services herself on account of everybody else fearing something awful would happen to them if they dared to cross through Sensabaugh Tunnel.

"Hand me another, would you?" Creed had stopped on the fifth rung of the ladder and was pointing to a stack of the tied-off lugs.

"All the talk about haints in that tunnel." Rain passed up a couple of the bundles. "There wasn't nothing to it."

"Yeah, how do you know? You ever been through that tunnel?"

"No."

"I didn't think so." Creed dropped a bundle over the wire stretched between two rafters. Using a long stick, he shoved that bundle across the furthest end of the wire, then dropped another. "If you think there's no truth to the rumors, how come you never go through the tunnel?"

"I never had a reason to." Rain finished tying off the last of the lugs.

"Well, I know there's haints in there."

"Is that so? I reckon you've seen them yourself?"

"No, I ain't seen 'em, but I've heard 'em."

"It's at times like these I am thankful I was hard of hearing."

"You should be. I went up there one time. That was all the convincing I needed. Soon as me and Brenda May got halfway through the tunnel, we heard a baby crying and a haint hollering, 'Turn back! Turn back!' So I put that Pinto in reverse and floored it."

Rain laughed at the thought of Creed's red Pinto flying backwards out of a dark hole in the mountainside. Carrying the last of the leaves, he climbed up the ladder and handed the tobacco to Creed.

"You know people say that the reason Burdy can pass through the tunnel unharmed is because it was her grandfather who strangled that baby in there all those years ago." Creed pushed the last bundle on the wire. "They say him's the one who haints the place. Him and that baby."

All this talk of Burdy was beginning to irritate Rain. He'd gone for a run to get shed of thinking about her. The last thing he wanted to do was ruminate with Creed about Burdy's so-called witching powers. He climbed back down the ladder. Creed followed.

"How's your daddy?" Rain asked, deciding to change the course of the conversation.

"Aww, he's alright, I reckon. His emphysema gives him trouble. He has to carry around the oxygen tank with him most every place he goes. He won't use it when he's out here, but if he goes to town, he takes it with him. He's uptown today. Said he had to go pay the light bill."

"Tell him I asked after him, would you? I'll try and get back up this way to see him before long."

"How long you going to be around for?" Creed asked.

"Longer than I planned."

"Say what?"

"I'm taking some time off work. Been a while since I've spent any time in these parts. Figured I could be a help to Burdy and catch up on some fishing and hiking."

It wasn't exactly lying. When he'd left Rhode Island, he was thinking he would do whatever was necessary to help Burdy. Of course, that was before he learned that Burdy had been betraying him all these years.

He had absolutely no intention now of helping Burdy Luttrell. Wheedin could stick her momma into one of those old peoples' homes until Burdy's mind turned to mush, or until she died and went on to Gloryland for all he cared. It was none of his concern. He wasn't about to give up a minute of his life worrying about the woman who had spent years deceiving him.

But he didn't make mention of that to Creed. The truth was too complicated even for Rain to ferret out. Sometimes, it's just easier to lie.

"I best be heading back," Rain said. "Got a long run ahead of me."

"You want me to give you a ride?" Creed offered. "The old pickup isn't much to look at, but she's pretty good at getting a person where they's headed."

"Mighty kind of you to offer, but I'm going to finish that run I started." Squatting down, Rain retied his shoes, taking care to double-knot the long laces. "Next time you're over my way, stop in. There's a couple quarts of peach shine left in the cupboards."

"I'll do that." Creed tipped his cap and waved as Rain headed off down the asphalt trail. Speaking to nobody but himself, Creed said, "I'll never understand why a man's got to run when there's nobody chasing him."

Chapter 8

A month had passed since the shooting at Bean Station, and Chief Conley was no closer to making an arrest in the case than he had been on that first day when the local undertaker came and hauled away the bodies of Hunk and Mary Nelle Kincer and Watson Loxley.

Conley had long grown tired of people pestering him about the investigation. He stopped eating at Minnie's, bringing his lunch to work or skipping it altogether, so he could avoid the public. He was glad he had already planned on retiring in the coming year. The public would tolerate an officer who banged his dispatch staff on company time, but they would never indulge a lawman who let a murderer run free.

Conley knew his failure to make an arrest had people questioning his abilities. Just last Sunday, he'd come out of the men's room at Union Avenue Methodist Church and overheard Paul Purdy tell Joyce Christian that the police sure were "dragging ass on this investigation." Those were his exact words—"dragging ass"—right there in the basement of the church. Why, if a person were to cut a hole in the ceiling where Paul Purdy was standing and cussing, they would be directly underneath the foot of the wooden cross hanging in the sanctuary. Of course, as soon as he seen Chief Conley, Paul fell mute.

"Morning, y'all," was the only thing Conley said as he brushed by Paul and Joyce.

"Morning, Chief," Joyce replied, while Paul nodded his head politely.

Conley didn't stick around to hear that morning's message. He walked right out the back door of the church and got into his cruis-

41

er. He didn't see no sense in driving his own rig when he was in town. Now, it would be a different story if he was headed to Nashville or Atlanta for pleasure. Not that he ever went anywhere anymore. The last family vacation he took was to Panama City Beach, Florida. That had to have been a decade or so ago, when Clive, his boy, was about fourteen or fifteen.

"Might've been even longer than that," Conley reflected. Killers weren't the only thing that got away from Chief Conley—time did too. He turned his cruiser north on Union Avenue, reaching over to grab his seat belt and buckling up.

Life in Bean Station made it easy for a lawman like Conley to forget how quickly the world was changing. The most recent crime-rate statistics out of the state proved once again that Bean Station was a pretty safe community to call home. Certainly much safer than Knoxville or Johnson City. Just because some dang fool went into Laidlow's and shot up four people, killing three of them, didn't automatically make Bean Station the murder capital of the Southeast. While it was true that burglaries and domestic violence were more commonplace than they had been five years ago, violent crimes were relatively rare in these parts.

Conley drove out Highway 11 toward Mooresburg, then cut up north on Highway 35 toward Sneedville. When Clive was a little fella, Chief Conley used to take his only boy up that way to fish the Upper Clinch. Clive's momma would always pitch a hissy fit on account of what she considered the dangers of the Upper Clinch.

"Foolishness," Conley said to himself as he remembered. The only danger along the River was getting wet or snake bit, but heck, a person around here could get snake bit walking in their backyard garden.

"I might should have paid more attention to it when he was younger," Conley mused as he popped in a cassette tape of Dolly Parton. He had a thing for Dolly, but what red-blooded man didn't?

"Clive," he answered himself. His son's choice of music was one of the many things that the two had argued over as Clive grew from a curious and kindly little boy into a surly and recalcitrant teenager. As a teen, Clive would spend untold hours alone in his room listening to the same Black Sabbath album again and again. Clive's mother had bought it against his father's protestations.

"Black Sabbath, really? Don't you find it an odd choice, giving the boy occult music for Christmas?" Conley had pressed when they went Christmas shopping together.

"It's what he wanted. See, it's right here." She pressed a torn piece of notebook paper into Conley's hand. Across the top, Clive had scrawled "Christmas list." The first item on the boy's list was a motorcycle. Conley huffed and handed the list back to his wife.

"Just because the album cover has a woman dressed like a witch doesn't mean it's Satan's music." She smugly placed the album in her shopping basket, next to the bag of bows and double-sided Scotch tape.

"Expert on the occult, now are you?" Conley mocked his wife as she walked away, heels clicking, waving her hand as she disappeared down the next aisle. He didn't press the issue over the record any further, but he had his reasons for worrying.

Six weeks prior, he'd attended a statewide caucus of law enforcement in Nashville to discuss an alarming rise of the occult among young kids. Investigators had given firsthand accounts of the connection between demonic and criminal activity.

One fellow from over at Soddy Daisy reviewed the highlights of a criminal case in which a fifteen-year old boy had hanged himself from the rafters of his family's barn. Police had suspected that the teen and his friends were responsible for a slew of animal abuse reports in the area. Two days before the boy took his life, remains of a goat that had been crudely slaughtered were found in a clearing not far from where the boy lived.

In the barn loft, the boy had built a rudimentary altar constructed of hay bales and river stones. He'd assembled the bones of what appeared to be various kills—a cat, a squirrel, a pig. There was even a cow's skull, though those were common on most farms.

The boy hadn't left a note, but he had used the pocketknife his grandfather had given him to carve crosses into the underside of each forearm. Until the medical examiner report confirmed it, investigators couldn't say for sure whether he'd died on account of the hanging or the blood loss. He had left behind some photos on that makeshift altar, disturbing pictures of himself dressed in a black monk-like robe, holding up some of the animals he'd killed, their necks sliced, blood dripping.

Conley thought it best not to mention any of that to his wife, but he couldn't help but notice that Clive displayed some of the same warning signs the investigators had highlighted: the isolation, the music, the surliness.

Clive never wanted to hang with his dad, or much of anyone else. He was no longer interested in fishing or hunting, things he had always loved as a young boy. Whenever Conley suggested it, Clive would give his dad this odd stare, like he was looking through him and not at him.

Pulling a cigarette from his shirt pocket, Conley pressed the knob of the car's lighter. He let the cigarette hang from his bottom lip till the lighter popped out fiery red, and then he lit it.

He'd started smoking that summer before Clive was born. Rolled his own cigarettes in those days. Everybody did. Tobacco was cheap. Clive had taken it up himself the summer before he started high school. Conley didn't like the boy smoking, but he hardly had grounds on which to argue against it. For a lawman, Conley was adverse to conflicts, especially those of a personal nature. Back then, the teen had a dog—a German shepherd named Bruiser—who ate cigarette butts like they was candy. Bruiser would wait until Clive took his last drag and mashed the butt underfoot, or flicked it from his fingers, then rush over and lick it up. Every time. It was the damndest thing, watching that dog wolf down those butts. Conley worried they'd make Bruiser sick, but they never did.

"They'll probably kill me one day, though," Conley said now as he drove across the Clinch River and headed on into Sneedville.

As he pulled his cruiser up in front of a yellow farmhouse, Conley noticed some ugly dark clouds drawing together directly above city hall. He decided then that his visit with Vaughnell Butry would have to be shorter than he'd planned. The last thing Conley needed today was to be stuck in a bad storm in Sneedville.

He knocked on the door. No answer. He knocked again, a little harder this time. Still no answer. He walked around back, stepping over a shovel in the side yard, then picking it up and leaning it against the house. Glancing through a tall window, Conley noticed the house was dark. No Trouble, Vaughnell's cat, brushed up against his leg, purring. Conley squatted down and scratched behind No Trouble's ears. "Where's Vaughnell at, old girl?" he asked.

"You looking for me?" Vaughnell Butry hollered out from between the rows of corn in her garden.

"There you are. I wondered where you were hiding."

"Not hiding, just working." Vaughnell stood up and waved at her cousin. She had the build of a dancer, long arms with well-defined muscles. She wore a black tank top underneath denim overalls, work boots, and flowered garden gloves. White hair, cut short, spiked out in all directions from underneath a red bandana. Her expressive brown eyes were shielded behind oversized sunglasses. "Whatcha doin' all the way up here on a Sunday?"

"Slumming."

"I can see that."

Conley went over and hugged her.

"I'm a sweaty mess," Vaughnell said, trying to keep Conley at arm's distance.

"Good gawd girl, you smell like a hog in heat."

"How would you know what a hog in heat smells like?"

"Now, that I can't tell you."

"Oh, I see. Cop secrets?"

Conley nodded. "Afraid so." Laughter erupted between the two. "I see somebody vandalized your sign out front."

"Gotta give them credit, that's some nice artwork, don't you think?"

Conley looked up the gravel driveway to the sign that usually proclaimed, "Sister Vaughnell: Palm Reader, Psychic and Spiritualist." Over her name in bright red letters, someone had painted the word "Quack." A huge cartoon duck covered the words "Psychic" and "Spiritualist."

"When did that happen?" Conley asked. He picked up the basket of corn and pole beans Vaughnell had gathered and carried it up to the back porch. Following him, she scooped up No Trouble and carried the calico in the crook of her arms, like an infant. No Trouble thought she'd died and gone to heaven. She clearly loved all that attention.

"Set that down right there and pull up a chair." Vaughnell nodded toward an old washing machine sitting by the back door. It had quit working long ago, but she wouldn't get shed of it. When Conley had offered to haul it to the dump, Vaughnell said there was still plenty of life in it. And as if to prove her point, she'd filled the washing bin full of dirt and planted geraniums in it.

Conley placed the basket by the washing machine turned planter. Grabbing a ladder-back chair, he turned it around and sat on it backwards so that he faced his cousin. "You didn't answer my question."

"Gimme a minute. I'm getting around to it," Vaughnell said. She pulled a flask from the front pocket of her overalls and took a sip, then reached out and offered it to Conley. He waved her off. "Suit yourself." Vaughnell took another long sip before tightening the cap and putting it back in her pocket. "Thursday morning as I was backing out of the drive. That's when I first noticed it. The women's club is helping spruce up the visiting room over at the Children's Advocacy Center. We're trying to make it more child friendly, less like an interrogation room, you know."

Conley wished to the Lord of all things holy that his cousin could just stick with the story, but Vaughnell was incapable of that. She had to go all the way around her elbow to get to her mouth.

"Well, I had to get over there before anyone else because I had all the paints and stencils for the zoo scene we was putting on the south wall," she continued. "Soon as I backed up out of my drive, I seen all that ugliness painted over my own sign. It made me late to my meeting."

"I'm sorry about that," Conley said.

"Yeah, me, too."

"Any idea who might have done it?"

"I'm a psychic. Of course I have some ideas who might've done it."

"Should I worry?"

"No," Vaughnell said. "Just some punk-ass kids. Nothing I can't handle myself."

"Good to know," Conley replied. The wind chimes hanging from a crepe myrtle were making a racket. A rainbow-inspired flag jutting from a post on the back porch wrapped around itself. "Wind picking up."

"Storm ain't far off now," Vaughnell agreed. "But you didn't come all this way just to hear about me." She pushed her sunglasses up on her head. Her brown eyes peered unflinchingly at Conley. "Was you needing something?"

"Yes," Conley said. "I need your help with a case I'm working."

"What kind of help?"

"I need you and those spirits of yours to help me track down the person who killed those people up at Laidlow's."

Chapter 9

Rain managed to avoid running into Burdy after she come home. It helped that she rarely left the house. Burdy was still using a walker, which made it difficult to get up and down either the front porch or the back one. Doc offered to build her a ramp to the back door, but she wouldn't have it. Burdy Luttrell had no intentions of accommodating a handicap of any sort. She intended to be walking good as new as quick as possible, and that's exactly what she said to Doc when he suggested the ramp. Until then, she spent the bulk of October inside doing the exercises the physical therapist recommended. The most she might do was sit on the porch shelling beans or visiting with whoever happened to be passing by or dropping in to check on her.

That suited Rain just fine. The few times she hollered at him to come join her on the porch, Rain just shined Burdy on, pretending like he didn't hear her and keeping on about his business. During the day he kept busy helping Doc replace the rotted wood in the barn on their property. Fact was, Doc and Leela-Ma didn't have much use for a barn anymore. They only kept one aged hog and one kindly mare now, and they didn't grow tobacco anymore.

Like most everybody else in the Bend, Doc and Leela had taken to buying their groceries uptown. Leela-Ma had deemed some time ago that she was done with butchering. She and Doc grew a few things in their garden still, but all their meat come from the grocer's icebox.

Leela had darn near managed to turn that remaining hog into a household pet. People around the Bend didn't think twice about that pig following Leela around all day long, but Rain thought it was the most confounding thing.

"What is she doing with that darn hog?" Rain inquired of Doc one morning as they were pulling rusted nails out of rotted timber on the barn's south side, closest to the pond.

"Watch your mouth, son," Doc replied. "You don't want Leela-Ma overhearing you cuss her baby."

"Baby? That hog must weigh nearly 300 pounds."

"Closer to 500, I'd venture," Doc said. He plopped a handful of rusty nails into a pail. "Hand me some of those, would you?" Doc pointed to the nails in a sack near Rain's boot.

"I can't believe Leela took up a hog as a house pet, naming it and everything."

"I'll tell you what, the name she gave it is a whole heap better than the name she first thunk up," Doc said. He pounded a couple of nails into the new board.

"Which was what?" Rain piled the rotted wood from the old barn into a heap. He wasn't at all sure he wanted to know what Leela-Ma had originally wanted to name a pig. He much preferred a simpler time when Leela and Doc just referred to all pigs as bacon.

"Thumbelina."

"Say what?"

"Thumbelina. She got it out of some story she read."

"I'm telling you, books are dangerous. This country ought to be more careful about who they entrust with ideas," Rain said. "Imagine if everybody went around thinking all the time."

"You let Leela hear you talk like that and she's liable to butcher you," Doc said. He wasn't laughing. "I think Leela saw something of herself in that story. A woman who couldn't have a child, so a fairy gives her some sort of magical barley seed that when planted becomes a girl, yay big." And with that Doc held up the end knuckle of his thumb. "Thumbelina. Get it?"

"Makes perfect sense," Rain said. "A hog as big as bale of hay and a girl half as big as your thumb have a lot in common."

"That's what I told her," Doc said. "She got put out with me making fun of her, so she come up with Abelshittim."

"Ableshittim? How is that a better name?" Rain yanked on a board that had rotted so badly only half of it was left. It gave away easily.

Doc laughed so hard he had to put his hammer down and wipe his eyes. "Don't worry. She shortened it to Abel. Besides, the name come straight out of the Bible. It was the forty-second encampment of the Israelites."

"Well, I guess that helps explain how come Abel waits for Leela by the side door of the church after prayer service then. As a creature near to the heart of God, I guess that hog feels pretty comfortable around the church house."

"More so than a lot of folks, I reckon."

"Me included," Rain said.

"Yeah, Leela told me to ask you about that."

"About what?" Rain said.

"About how come you ain't been to church since you been back in the Bend."

Rain thought it was good fortune when, at that moment, Ida Mosely honked the horn on her old Dodge pickup and waved as she rounded the corner of Christian Bend and Miller's Bluff roads. Rain had been meaning to get up to Ida's place for a visit but hadn't done it yet. He hadn't done a lot of things he'd intended to do when he first come back home. Ever since he'd discovered those letters, he didn't feel like seeing anybody or being seen by anybody. So far, Rain had avoided speaking about what was troubling him. He intended to keep it that way. "Ain't it about time for lunch?" he asked.

It was only 10:45, and lunch was at least a good half-hour or more away, but Doc understood that it wasn't hunger that was bothering Rain. Something else was. Something Rain clearly had no mind to speak of.

Doc stood up, slowly, his back aching something awful. His knees, too. Some days Doc felt like he ought to carry around a can of WD-40 so he could oil all the joints that went crickety on him throughout the day. "C'mon. There's some pork chops and a couple slices of apple pie left over from last night's dinner."

"Who has pie left over?" Rain asked. He was smiling as he followed Doc across the yard and around the back of the house, where the two of them stopped by the outside spigot to wash up.

"Well, it sure wasn't me," Doc said. "If Leela hadn't been acting like the food police, I would have eat the whole pie last night."

Chapter 10

Kade Mashburn knew about the shooting at Laidlow's. Hell, who didn't? It was the daily headline until Tennessee tied Auburn as some 100,000 fans went bat-shit crazy in Neyland Stadium. Typically, Kade avoided crowds, unless, of course, he was playing before one. But he hadn't picked up his guitar, much less played before a crowd, in years. It wasn't any one thing that had caused him to put his guitar away. If Kade had learned anything from his line of work, it was that dreams don't die abruptly; they suffer from chronic neglect.

He'd played the juke joint circuit for years, trying to make a name for himself and succeeding in some people's eyes, albeit never his own. He'd cut a couple of records, even, but after the second one failed to sell more than a thousand copies, his label dropped him. Kade didn't blame his agent for the label's actions. Phil had done everything within his power to sell Kade, short of sleeping with Naomi Judd, and Phil was even willing to do that if Naomi ever asked. For whatever reason, Kade just couldn't find traction in Nashville, much less a broader market.

"It's a crying shame," Phil had said. "You're one of the most talented songwriters I've ever signed. Keith Whitley called me this morning to say how much he's going to miss working with you."

"That's nice of him," Kade replied.

"I feel like I failed you. Maybe all you need is a different agent."

"Phil, listen, you've done nothing but believe in me and I appreciate that more than I can ever put into words. It's just not in the cards, man. For whatever reason I am lacking that 'it' factor you fellas are always talking about. I could keep hanging around Nashville, kicking an empty can, but what if I never break through? I can't keep chasing this. A fella ought to have more than one dream, anyhow."

"So what are your other dreams?" Phil asked.

"I don't know yet," Kade said. "It's hard, living in Nashville, to think of any dream beyond bright lights and a stage. That's how come I'm leaving."

Phil and Kade both knew there was more to his decision than Kade was letting on.

Since coming to Nashville, Kade had buried more than one friend from overdoses. It always started out the same: a little harmless pot smoking, a little too much drinking, a lot of cocaine, a lot more meth, and, to recover from all that, prescription opiates. The latter usually killed them.

And the most recent death was the hardest on Kade. Travis Greene, an ambitious kid out of Tifton, Georgia, was just twenty-six years old when Kade found him dead in a hotel bed. They'd played together at the Station Inn on numerous occasions. Rory Madden had a special fondness for the spirited singer, telling Greene he reminded him ever so much of Bob Montgomery, Buddy Holly's sidekick and writing partner. Everyone who heard him perform at the Station Inn predicted that it wouldn't be long before Greene would be the featured artist on the Opry stage.

Kade never even knew Greene had a drug problem. One of the biggest issues with addicts was that they looked like regular folks. Hell, addicts were regular folks: the pastor at First United, the Little League coach, the gal selling Mary Kay, the pediatrician next door, the cheery clerk in the mayor's office. What child grows up hoping to become an addict?

Kade wasn't sure if Greene had come to Nashville with a drug problem or if the drug problem was the result of his coming to Nashville. Not that it made any difference. But still, Kade couldn't help feeling guilty. Had he only known, he would have gotten the kid some help. Maybe saved the boy's family back in Georgia a whole lot of heartache. But a person can't know what they don't know, and Greene never showed any outward signs of having a problem.

Kade had grown tired of Nashville, anyway. The bright lights had lost their glimmer. He'd rather walk the banks of the Holston on a moonlit night. He'd rather eat cold chicken on the porch with Doc than another plate of Prince's hot chicken alone. He'd grown homesick for East Tennessee before, but Greene's death undid him. Whatever romantic notions Kade once held about the city and a career in country music faded against the neon backlight of McCullers Funeral Home sign.

Before they shut the casket lid on the kid from Tifton, Kade made a promise to himself as much as to Travis Greene. He would find a way to make a difference. He would do his level best to keep others from falling into the same dark well. Kade made good on his promise when he packed up his belongings the next month and headed for Knoxville, where he got a job as a baggage carrier at the airport and entered the University of Tennessee. Midway through his degree program, he got hired on with the Drug Enforcement Agency.

Now here it was 1987, and despite the hundreds of cases he'd worked over the years, the drug problem in Tennessee was growing at a mercurial rate. Kade felt like he'd jumped a sinking ship only to land in the ocean without a life vest. Whatever illusions he had back at McCullers Funeral Home about righting the wrongs of young kids overdosing were rolled up and smoked long since.

Kade Mashburn had managed to hang on to his rugged good looks, but not the two wives those looks had given him. He'd left his first wife behind in Nashville. Well, to be clear, she'd left him before they celebrated their first-year anniversary. Julia claimed she was going to a tailgate party in The Grove before Ole Miss's first home game that year. When she didn't return even after the football season ended, Kade went over to the courthouse and filed for divorce.

The next marriage was even shorter. It ended as soon as Kade discovered that Andrea, the beautiful brunette he'd met at Ault's Bar on Main, wasn't quite divorced from her first husband. Something Kade didn't realize until a Samoan man, with clenched fists big as boxing gloves, pounded on the door of the honeymoon suite of Atlanta's Ritz-Carlton shortly after Kade had carried his new bride and the other man's wife over the threshold.

Kade could laugh about the brevity of both marriages now, and he often did after a few beers, but that didn't keep him from cursing anyone who suggested that they knew the "perfect girl" for him. Which is exactly what happened when his buddy Larry invited Kade to join him and his wife, Pam, for an early Halloween celebration. Larry hadn't said anything about the possibility of Pam bringing along a friend. He'd just told Kade they'd meet him at Suttree's at 7 p.m.

An upscale restaurant located on the riverfront, Suttree's was the kind of place Kade usually avoided. Partial to Cracker Barrel's microwaved mac and cheese, he was a bit surprised when Larry first suggested the steak-and-lobster joint, and started to balk until Larry mentioned that it was Pam's favorite. Kade had a soft spot for Larry's wife. Something about her seemed fragile, reminding him of the way Maizee had been all those years ago. Larry had confided in Kade that the reason he and Pam didn't have any children is because she'd suffered through three miscarriages before giving birth to a stillborn. After that the couple quit trying.

Larry and Pam were already seated at one of the outside tables when Kade arrived, late as usual.

"Sorry," Kade said, noticing the spinach dip, half eaten, and Larry's nearly empty glass of bourbon.

Pam stood up and gave Kade a hug. "No worries. We've just been sitting here enjoying the river people." She nodded toward a leather-skinned man fishing with a cane pole and a scrawny woman with melon breasts falling out of her red tank top sitting on an overturned bucket.

"Always lots of interesting scenery down here," Kade said.

Larry shook Kade's hand. "Glad you could make it. I wasn't sure when I called if you'd be in town." Even at the end of the day, Larry's standard white shirt held its starch and boasted monogrammed cufflinks—LWW. Larry Wayne Wiltshire.

A waiter came and took Kade's drink order, whiskey straight. Pam pushed the spinach dip his way.

"No thanks," Kade said. "I try never to eat before drinking. Don't need the extra calories." He patted his taut abs mockingly.

"Yeah, that's a problem for you alright." Pam rolled her green eyes and laughed. A light breeze coming off the river blew her blond bangs up. Patting them back into place, Pam said, "I have a little surprise for you."

"Oh, yeah?" Kade said, his eyebrows raised.

Larry moaned audibly.

"What kind of surprise?" Kade asked.

"A lovely one," Pam replied. "Just wait, and you'll see." She unfolded a napkin and handed it to Kade as the waiter placed his whiskey on the table and handed Larry his second bourbon.

"Thank you," Kade said, accepting the green napkin and placing it across his lap.

A car on the bridge honked, and the driver waved to the man fishing below. The busty woman picked up her bucket and moved it over three feet. Kade reflected that sometimes a person just needs a different perspective from which to view the river.

"Have you had a chance to look over the menu?" the waiter asked. Kade noticed that the young man's black slacks were frayed around the hem—likely the only pair of dress pants he owned. A college student no doubt. Working his way through UT.

"We are still waiting for a friend," Pam said. "But I'll take another chardonnay." She handed the kid her glass.

"Of course, ma'am." The waiter took the glass. "I'll be right back."

As he walked away, Kade turned to Pam. "My surprise, huh? So who's joining us?"

He knew his annoyance was obvious, so he focused on Larry, who was slumped comfortably in his chair, legs crossed, his blue eyes rolling in that "Oh, Brother, here we go now" fashion.

"A lovely gal," Pam insisted. "We've only recently met. She's not from around here. She's from somewhere up North. Boston, maybe? Or Baltimore? Are they close to one another?"

"Depends on what you mean by close," Larry said. "Do you mean close as in the Texas way or in that South Carolina manner?" He winked at Pam.

"I got that wrong. I think it's one of those other B-towns. Brooklyn? Yes. I think it's Brooklyn. Is that the one near Philly?"

"Never mind her," Larry said. "She's always been a little directionally challenged."

"Mother pointed out the same thing when I decided to marry you," Pam said. "She said I was lacking in life direction hooking up with the likes of you." Pam flashed both men a bright smile. She loved a witty retort, whether hers or anybody's.

While Larry came from a perfectly respectable family, Pam had definitely married "down." The former Lady Vols all-star was the daughter of Knoxville's mayor, Ridley Wofford. Her daddy had made a bid for governor. He lost, but his good buddy, Lamar Alexander, gave him an appointment that translated to money and power. It was all a little much for Kade. He emptied his glass. "I really wish you would give me a heads up before you arrange dates for me."

"If she did that, you'd never show up," Larry said.

"Exactly," Kade agreed.

"Would you two stop?" Pam knew it was a risk, setting Kade up like this, but he left her no choice. Had she called him ahead of time and told him she'd met the perfect girl for him, Kade would have blown her off. And Pam didn't care what Kade said about not having room in his life for a woman, being unlucky in love, and all that jazz; she knew the problem was that Kade hadn't met the right woman yet. She felt it was her duty to make sure he did. It was a job she assumed with the rigor of Pat Summit, her former basketball coach.

"Don't worry," Larry said. "We will be true southern gentlemen, won't we, Kade?" He sat back in his chair, straightened his tie, ran his hand through his brown bangs, and then fiddled with his cufflinks. "How do you like your blue-eyed boy now, Mrs. Reaper?"

Pam leaned over and kissed Larry on the cheek.

Kade flipped Larry the bird and excused himself. "Sorry, guys, I need to go drain my lizard."

"Tie a string to it and hold it," Pam ordered. "You can't leave now. That's her there." Pam pointed to a petite gal with shoulder-length brown hair talking to the hostess. She wore a pink floral dress that reminded Kade of something Goldie Hawn might have worn. She had the figure of a teenager, small of hip and waist, perky breasted. Kade had to admit that, at least this time around, Pam had managed to find someone who captured his attention. The gal turned toward them and smiled nervously. Pam waved and called out, "Thomasina! Over here!"

Chapter 11

When Clint was unable to reach Burdy on that first Saturday, he didn't worry. It had happened on occasion over the years; one of them would get tied up with something and be unable to make the call. The six-hour time difference sometimes messed them up. When the call came, Clint would usually pour himself a glass of wine after dinner and sit on the patio while talking with Burdy, who was most often cleaning up the dishes from her lunch.

They would talk about the usual things lovers talk about, the little things: who they saw in town; what books they were reading; the latest political scandal—between the leaders in France and the United States, there was always some political scandal—the latest thing blooming in the garden, and, as always, how much they missed each other and couldn't wait to see one another again.

Between Burdy's twice-a-year trips to Bayeux and Clint's four-times-a-year trips to Washington, D.C., or Atlanta, they'd managed to see each other on a fairly regular basis. That first trip to France had been Burdy's most challenging, but it gave her the confidence she needed to make the trips alone after that. She only went twice more by ship. Planes proved to be a lot more practical, and if Burdy was anything, she was practical.

After the first couple of years, people in the Bend quit inquiring about where she was headed off to. They just figured that Burdy, like all of them, needed to visit family that had moved off. Besides, in those early years, her work at the TB hospital up at Pressmen's Home gave her ample reason to scoot off down to Atlanta or up to D.C. whenever she wanted. Burdy would tell folks that she was going for training or research or some such thing.

There was a fine TB sanatorium just outside of Atlanta and couple in D.C.

Clint was recalling one of those Atlanta getaways when he picked up the phone to call Burdy the following week. He was thinking it had to be the time in 1962 because of the news headlines about the Reds backing down on Cuba. Sipping on a glass of Bordeaux, he waited for Burdy to pick up on the other end.

Only she never did.

The phone rang and rang and rang some more. Burdy didn't use an answering machine. She didn't figure she needed one. Anyone in the Bend who wanted to get a hold of her knew to ring her up or just holler real loud for her—she'd come a'running. Burdy didn't need or want a machine keeping track of her life. She could manage it just fine, thank you very much.

After eight or nine rings, Clint hung up. He finished his glass of wine and poured another before trying the number again. By the time he took the last sip of that second glass, he'd called Burdy's number four times. Each time she failed to answer, Clint grew increasingly worried. In all the years that had passed between them, Burdy had always been faithful to their scheduled calls.

Now this. Two missed scheduled calls.

Picking up his glass and the near-empty bottle of wine, Clint carried them to the kitchen. He rinsed the glass and wiped it with a cloth. Staring out the window, he noticed that the stone angel sitting beside the pots of red geraniums had a broken wing. How had that happened? When had it happened? Why hadn't the gardener made any mention of it? Clint dried his hands and walked outside.

Leaning over the three-foot statue, he felt between the angel and the privacy wall for the missing wing. He walked all along the wall, rustling through the manicured boxwoods and flowerbeds, searching. It wasn't there.

The angel had been a gift from Burdy. She'd picked it up at Mathilde Antiquities, a local shop on Rue Larcher, the day after

Clint first asked her to marry him in September of '59. Although he could no longer remember the number of times Burdy had turned down his repeated proposals over the years, he would never forget that first time. He thought he would never recover from the grief of her rejection.

They had spent the day wandering the cobbled streets of Arromanches. When the sun was high overhead, they sat on a concrete bench, ate sausages laden with mustard, and talked about how even in war there are shining moments of creativity. They could see Mulberry Harbour in the distance. The temporary piers, first imagined and sketched out by Winston Churchill, had been used by Allied Forces to offload troops, cargo, and vehicles.

Burdy and Clint walked out to the piers that had served as the thoroughfare for the Allies. Moss-covered steel pilings stretched out like the backbone of a prehistoric reptile into the waters flowing between the coasts of France and England.

"Can you imagine driving a tank over that?" Burdy asked as she stood before the massive structure.

"Not even a jeep," Clint replied.

Burdy slipped off her sandals at the water's edge. She was wearing a paisley scarf tied underneath her chin. Clint noticed that the aqua of her eyes was made even more brilliant by the purple-and-green cloth. She wasn't beautiful in any conventional way, but it was those Melungeon looks of hers—the long, dark hair, the brown complexion, the bright eyes—that made Burdy lovelier than all the women of France. Sometimes, like in this moment, Clint found it almost impossible to look away. He was in love with Burdy Luttrell and knew that he always would be.

"What are those people doing over there?" Burdy asked, seeming oblivious to his adoration. She pointed at a group gathering in a circle up the beach, away from the piers and the foamy waters. They were eyeing something in the sand. A crab maybe? A jellyfish? Some strange sea creature beached?

"I don't know," Clint said, shrugging. A child—Clint couldn't tell if it was a boy or a girl—ran in front of them, chasing a small white dog who was running after a red ball.

"They're digging at something," Burdy said. "They've got a hoe or rake. Let's walk over that away." She turned and Clint followed, carrying her sandals. The group moved a few feet south. Then a few feet east. Then again to the south. Then again to the east. The whole time they circled around somebody who was using what they could now see was indeed a rake.

"They're raking the sand," Burdy said, stopping just shy of the group.

"I see that," Clint replied. He handed Burdy her sandals. Holding Clint's forearm to steady herself, Burdy slipped her shoes back on.

"Can you make out what it is?" she asked.

"Looks like they are using a pattern of some sort, cardboard or something. See that?" Clint pointed to a man in the crowd who was kneeling over what appeared to be a silhouette of a person.

"Go ask one of them what they're doing," she urged.

"Why?"

"Because I want to know," Burdy said. The circle moved their pattern to another spot a few feet from the one they'd just raked.

"Then you go ask," Clint said. "I'll wait for you." He flashed her a grin.

"Very gentlemanly of you," she said, mocking annoyance.

"You are the curious one. I'm happy not knowing about a lot of things."

"Aren't you the same fellow who served with the Resistance during the war? Didn't you make it your business to know more than others?" Burdy asked. Seagulls squawked overhead, playing happy audience to her quick retort.

"Which is why I am perfectly happy not knowing anything during peaceful times," Clint replied. "I'll wait right here."

"Suit yourself," Burdy said, turning away and walking over to the crowd, which had moved again.

"Excuse me," she said to a woman wearing a navy windbreaker and holding a clipboard. The woman turned. Burdy noticed she had a kind face. "You look like somebody official. Can you tell me what's going on here?"

The woman smiled. "Oui," she answered. "We are artists, and this," she stretched out her arms to indicate the beach, "is our canvas."

Burdy glanced up and down the beach. "That's a lot to work with."

"Oui," the woman nodded. "It is good. We will require it all."

"So what are you creating?"

"Dead people," the woman replied.

"Dead people?" Burdy asked, completely befuddled.

The woman nodded, then made a mark on her clipboard as the group moved a few more feet over and put the pattern in the sand again. Burdy could now see that the outline was that of a person, fallen and splayed out. "We are replicating the 9,000 men who died on these beaches," the woman said.

Burdy was quiet. Sometimes silence is the best response. This was one of those times.

"Excuse me," the lady with the kind face said. "I am falling behind. I must stay with my group."

"Yes," Burdy said. "Yes, of course. I'm sorry I distracted you."

The woman waved as she walked away. "Merci. All is well. Please come back when we have finished."

Burdy and Clint did return that evening just before sunset. Standing on the jetty looking out across the beach, they scanned the thousands of bodies etched in the sand by volunteers intent on helping people remember the lives lost during the American invasion at Normandy.

"It's a miracle anyone got out alive," Burdy whispered.

"It is," Clint agreed. He knew that Burdy was thinking of one person in particular—Zeb. And while it was true that Zeb made it out alive, Clint sometimes wondered about the diminished life the American had now. Zeb had lost his wife, his son, and his home. The burden of that loss seemed too great a price. What kind of freedom had all that loss earned Zeb?

A sharp wind cut across the jetty. Burdy shivered. Clint put his arm around her, pulled her to him tightly. A wave rolled in and washed away some of the sand, erasing the bodies with it. They stood locked into a quiet embrace, rocking one another as they watched the tide carry away the imaginary bodies of soldiers they never knew, thinking about the one they did know. For a very long time, neither said anything.

Then, finally, Clint reached into his coat pocket and pulled out a small box. Inside was his mother's wedding ring. He'd already had it resized for Burdy. He flipped open the lid on the box and held it in front of them both.

"Marry me," he said.

"Oh, Clint." Burdy sighed. She reached out, took the ring from its velvet bed, and slipped it over her finger. This was no ordinary ring, and she knew it. It was a family heirloom passed down for generations.

"Marry me," Clint said again, kissing her forehead.

Burdy said nothing but turned the two-carat solitaire around so that it captured the colors of the setting sun.

"It's a Tiffany," he said. "One of the first. Grand-pere was friends with Charles Tiffany. He helped him establish his shop in Paris. *Grand-mère* Amelie lost it once."

"Lost it?" The thought terrified Burdy. She started to slip the ring off, return it to its velvet bed.

"No!" Clint said. "Leave it!" His tone startled Burdy. She kept the ring on. "*Grand-mère* wore it while sewing. It fell off as she was stuffing pillows. It was caught by the duck feathers and remained in one of the pillows until she died. After, when her maid cut all the pillows open and removed the feathers, she found the ring and returned it to my papa."

"It is a lovely ring," Burdy said, holding out her hand and admiring the elegance it gave her stubby finger.

"Marry me."

The wind blew the scarf back, and Burdy's hair danced every which way. Clint reached over and pulled the scarf back into place, tucking her flyaway hair beneath it. "I love you, Burdy Luttrell. I always will. Marry me. S'il vous plaît."

Burdy pulled Clint's head to her own and kissed him longingly, slowly. He tasted of sun and saltwater. She pressed her breasts against him. He wrapped his arms around her and pulled her back in until there was no breeze between them. They ignored the stares of passersby, the gulls squawking overhead, and the encroaching tide. In each other's arms there was no other world, only them, only their's.

They might have remained in that space until dark fell if not for the drunken bicyclist who crashed into a parked car on the street behind them with a startling noise. They saw that the cyclist was passed out, and not from drinking. His head was bleeding profusely. Clint rushed over and pressed a hanky to the cyclist's forehead to staunch the flow of blood.

"Lord a' mercy," Burdy said. All she'd been able to do was hand him the handkerchief. She might have done more if this accident had happened at home in the Bend, but here in France Burdy recognized her place as the outsider. When a gal can't speak the language of a country, it leaves her feeling a mite unsure about what she does know. On the streets of Arromanches, she feared her healing powers wouldn't be welcomed.

Two flics came running down the street from the corner station. One carried a first-aid bag. Clint moved aside as soon as they arrived.

"I think he'll be okay," Clint reassured Burdy as he stopped to wash his hands in the public drinking fountain. "It's mostly a surface cut. Head injuries always bleed badly. I don't think he'll remember a thing when he comes to. He'd anesthetized himself a good deal beforehand."

Burdy waited until they'd walked away from the gathering crowd of looky-loos before taking off the ring Clint had given her. "Much as I might wish otherwise, I can't marry you," she told him, placing the ring into his palm.

"Can't or won't?" he asked. The sharpness in his tone did not surprise Burdy. She knew her refusal would hurt him, and while she hated that, she did what she thought was best for the both of them.

"Maybe a bit of both," she replied. "I love you, Clint. You are the first man I have allowed myself to love since Tibbis died, but how can I marry you? Your life is here in France. Mine is in Tennessee. I can't leave the Bend. It's all I've ever known. And I won't ask you to leave your life here to join me there. It's not right. These are your people. My people are across the ocean." She was crying, softly, upset that she had to deny Clint and herself a future together.

Finding love wasn't easy—Burdy could attest to that—but once found it was no guarantee that a person got to hang on to it. Burdy only had to look to the beach behind her to see proof of that. Among those killed on D-Day were husbands, fiancés, boyfriends, and beaus-in-the-making. Burdy just had to recall Zeb and Maizee's own fragile love story to know that the one central truth about true love is that it sure enough will break a person's heart in a million different ways.

"Ask me," Clint said. He cupped his hand underneath her chin, caught her tears.

"Say what?" Burdy looked up at him, confused.

"Ask me."

"Ask you what?"

"Ask me to come to Tennessee. I'll do it. I will. I promise. If you'll marry me. Right now. Tomorrow. Next week. Whenever. Just say yes, Burdy. I'll leave France for you." Clint's bushy brows pinched together. His eyes reflected his earnest heart.

Burdy looked down. "I can't ask you to do that. I can't. You would grow to resent me, and I could never bear that."

"No I wouldn't," Clint said. "I love you, Burdy. I could never resent you." But his voice lacked conviction. They both heard it.

"I can't ask you that, Clint. I won't."

He placed the sparkling ring back into the box, flipped the lid closed, and slipped it into his pocket.

"Then we will find our happiness in the moments we do have together, however few or however many," he said. He took Burdy's hand into his own and gave it a squeeze.

Clint would continue to ask Burdy to marry him over the years, but her answer never changed. And while they'd figured out ways to be together as often as possible, those ways had never included an invitation from Burdy for Clint to come to the Bend.

Zeb asked Clint once how come he didn't just up and marry Burdy, and he told him the honest truth: "She won't have me."

"What do you mean she won't have you?" Zeb asked.

Clint explained Burdy's reasoning as best he could. Zeb said he could see how Burdy might think that way. At one time, he'd thought that he could never leave the Bend to live anywhere else, but the war had changed all that, had changed him so much it was impossible for him to ever return.

"You don't mean that," Clint had replied.

"But I do," Zeb insisted. "I'll never go home again."

"Never is a very long time."

"I know." Zeb gulped back black coffee and crushed the empty Styrofoam cup in one hand before tossing it in the trash.

"Wouldn't you like to see your son again?"

Zeb had stared out the windows for a while before answering. "No," he said finally.

Clint let it go. He knew from his talks with Burdy that war had changed Zeb, made him think about things in ways that were different from the thoughts of people who'd never been to war. There was a lot about Zeb that didn't make any sense to Clint.

Burdy always saw Zeb on her visits to France. They would usually have a couple of meals together during her week in town. Sometimes Clint would join them, but most often not. Zeb wasn't open to forming a relationship with Clint, no matter how much Clint tried. Even when Burdy wasn't in town, Clint would drop by the bistro where Zeb worked, have a sandwich and some coffee, try to befriend him. But Zeb made it clear that he wasn't looking for a friendship. He'd chat for a minute and then always find some reason to excuse himself: dishes to wash, cucumbers to slice, floors to sweep. After a few years, Clint quit trying. Whatever trauma Zeb was dealing with remained nameless. Clint knew that the demons encountered in war were some of the most violent, which explained why the suicide rates among veterans remained high long after most wars ended.

After three Saturdays passed and Clint still couldn't reach Burdy by phone, Zeb was the first person he sought out. Who else could he turn to? No one in the Bend knew him or even anything about "the Frenchman." Nobody knew Burdy had a lover.

Clint found Zeb at the bibliothèque reading the current issue of TIME magazine. It was Zeb's routine to head out to the bibliothèque every Wednesday after his mid-morning coffee. He'd spend most of the day there, catching up on all the local and world news and reading whatever author happened to interest him that week.

Lately, he'd been plowing through Proust as best he could. In the early years, Father Thom had encouraged Zeb to learn French. He'd even hired a tutor to work with him. After decades of studying, Zeb could read French almost as well as he could English, which wasn't to say he'd mastered either one, really. But forty years of working in the bistro and living in the community of Bayeux had ensured that Zeb could speak the language nearly as well as the locals.

"Tenez!" Clint said softly as he walked up to Zeb.

"Tu m'a cherchè?" Zeb looked up from his book, startled by Clint's greeting.

"J'ai cherchè presque tout le batiment pour vous." Clint's white hair curled out over his ears like wings, giving the appearance that he was about to take flight. His hair and a little rounding of his shoulders were the only concessions to aging. Clint was still a good-looking fellow.

"Qu'est-ce qui se-passe?" Zeb noticed the redness in Clint's face, the tightness to his jaw, the way sweat made his hair curl. It was clear to Zeb that Clint was agitated.

Clint pulled out a chair and leaned forward, his hands folded on the table between them. "I can't get in touch with Burdy!" he blurted out, switching to Zeb's native tongue to be sure Zeb understood the urgency. "I call her the same times each week, and sometimes we miss each other but rarely. It's been nearly a month since we last spoke, and I'm worried that something terrible has happened to her."

"Whoa, there, slow down." Clint had spoken so fast, Zeb wasn't sure he'd grasped the point. "So you can't get ahold of Burdy?"

"No," Clint said.

"When's the last time you spoke?"

Clint rubbed his hands together, and his eyes darkened. "It's been at least three weeks, maybe four. I've called nearly every day this past week, but the phone just rings and rings. I can't remember if we spoke last in August or early September, but we have never gone this long without talking. Never."

Zeb didn't like what he was hearing. Burdy was up in years. The likelihood that something awful had happened to her was a very real possibility, but Zeb didn't want to upset Clint any further.

"You didn't have a falling out or anything like that? An argument? She's not sore with you over something?"

Clint put his palms flat on the table and stared directly at Zeb. "No," he said. "Nothing like that." He spoke in a firm and authoritative way that made it clear to Zeb he thought the idea of falling out was ludicrous.

"I'm sorry," Zeb said. "I had to ask. We shouldn't jump to conclusions, shouldn't think the worst."

But of course they both were thinking the same thing—if Burdy up and died, how would either of them know? There would be no one to call and tell them. Wheedin, like everybody else in the Bend, had long ago assumed Zeb dead. And Burdy had told no one about Clint, ever.

"What should we do, then?" Clint asked. "What should we do?"

Zeb was silent for a long while. He knew what needed to be done; he just couldn't bring himself to say it aloud.

Clint, despite trying not to, feared the worst. He knew in his heart of hearts that the only thing that would keep Burdy from answering his calls, or not calling him, was if she was unable to do so. She was either disabled or dead, and neither was an option that Clint could handle. He sucked in a deep breath, trying to control the panic, but when he exhaled it came out in big, heaving sobs. He buried his face in his hands.

Zeb reached across the table and patted the old chap's forearm. "It's going to be okay, Clint. It is. We'll go to the Bend together. We'll find her, wherever she is. I promise. We'll find Burdy. Don't worry. I'm sure everything will be just fine."

Zeb didn't believe for one minute that everything would be fine. In fact, he could hardly believe what he was saying. What would happen if he returned to the Bend after all these years? Still, he knew he owed it to Burdy, who had done nothing but love and care for his wife and boy for so long. If Burdy was dead, Zeb needed to know as much as Clint did—even if knowing required returning to Tennessee, a trip he'd dreaded since the day he shot and killed that French boy in the field in Sainte-Mère-Église.

Chapter 12

Smoke rose from the chimney on the house over the hill from Boog McPheeter's place. Boog knew that the old man who lived there had a difficult time keeping warm since the doctors put him on blood thinners. The old man used to sit on the porch and wave at the neighbors as they rode up and down the road. Nowadays the fellow could be found sitting inside on most any day, with his chair pulled close to the wood stove.

Not Boog. He couldn't stand to be cooped up inside a house all day long like that. He told his boy Creed and anybody else within earshot that he'd much rather die alone in the woods than take a medicine that made him so cold he couldn't get outside no more. Boog had grown up in these hills, and there was no better time to enjoy them than in the month of October.

Sometimes ignorant people who didn't know any better would belittle the University of Tennessee's choice of school colors. They thought UT's orange looked like something road workers wore. Not Boog. He loved that bright, bold orange. In October, when the trees on the mountains turned so many shades of orange, it hurt a fella's eyes to look, especially under the glare of midday. No matter how intense that orange might be, a fellow just couldn't look away from all that beauty. Well, at least Boog couldn't.

He was standing in the gravel drive, finishing his smoke, looking up at the mountains, when Creed come up the road, driving way too fast as usual. Boog stomped out the cigarette. He wasn't supposed to smoke. Doctor said it would only aggravate his emphysema. Boog found the doctor aggravating, but he got rid of the cigarette anyway. He knew Creed would start hollering at him about it if he didn't.

Creed hadn't come home all night. Boog had no idey where his boy was or what he was doing, but he was pretty damn sure Creed was up to no good. If Boog were to drop dead from heart problems, more than likely they'd be brought on by Creed, not some clot or even one of Boog's coughing fits. Some children are born to honor their parents, and others are born to vex them. Creed was the vexing sort. There wasn't a prayer prayed or a threat uttered that could curb Creed from following a crooked path. He was hell-bent for trouble. Always had been.

"Fine morning," Boog said as Creed stepped out of the rig. Boog wondered when Creed last bathed. His naturally golden hair was a dirty shade of brown, long, unruly, and unkempt. He smelled of day-old beer and God only knows what else. Boog knew Creed smoked the weed. He had a patch of it growing out behind the house in a sunny pinch of land. Lawmen didn't run these parts too much, but if they did, they wouldn't see it no-how.

Boog didn't like it one bit. He told Creed the weed would turn a good man into a lazy no-count. He'd witnessed that more times than he cared to discuss, especially with his own son. But Creed was a stubborn cuss and not prone to paying any respect to his old man, especially if it conflicted with what he wanted to do. And what Creed really wanted to do was make money without having to work hard at it. Weed was a better cash crop than tobacco and not nearly as much work. Maybe his daddy was right about the lazy part, but Creed saw no reason for a man to work as hard as his daddy had. Boog wouldn't have half the health problems if he hadn't had to work so hard.

Creed rubbed his eyes with the butt of his hand, hacked up a snot-ball and spit it out. Then did it again.

"Rough night?" Boog asked. He was annoyed with Creed but tried not to be.

"No, not really," Creed said. He pulled a cigarette from his shirt pocket and cupped his hand around the tip as he lit it. It took a few tries to get a flame going on the cheap convenience store lighter. He took a long drag and leaned against the tire wheel of his daddy's old pickup. "You headed someplace?"

Boog was shaven and wearing his gray felt hat, not the straw gardening one. "Yeah."

"Where?"

"The police chief up at Bean Station wants to see me."

"Why would the police up at Bean Station want to see you?" A shadow passed over Creed's face, momentarily giving him a menacing look. Boog looked up, saw a kettle of turkey buzzards overhead.

"Said he wants to see me about that shooting that happened last month."

Creed moved away from the rig, pulled himself up to his full height of 6'2", like a drill sergeant had called him to attention or something. "Yeah, I remember hearing something about that. Is that the same one where Burdy Luttrell got shot?"

"I suspect so," Boog said. "Far as I know, that's been the only shooting at Bean Station since Daniel Boone passed on." Boog was trying to make light of the situation. Creed might let on like he didn't know about the shooting at the pharmacy, but Boog could tell the whole conversation was making his boy nervous for some reason.

Creed pinched off the end of his cigarette and flicked it out towards the road. "You want me to drive you up there?"

"You don't look like you got much sleep last night. I think you better go on to the house and try to catch up."

"Suit yourself," Creed said. "But you better take your oxygen with you." Boog knew that Creed wasn't saying this out of concern for him, but rather to remind him of his limitations. Creed was sadistic that way. He wasn't shy about reminding his daddy that he had more brute strength. He could be a creepy fellow sometimes. This was one of those times.

"I appreciate your looking out for me," Boog replied. "I'll be sure and do that." He didn't even try and hide the snipe in his comeback. He might not be as physically strong as Creed, but he sure the hell was a lot more quick-witted than his addled-minded son.

Creed didn't bother showering or shaving. He went to the kitchen and poured himself a cup of lukewarm coffee from the pot his father had made earlier that morning. Then, he sat on the front stoop, smoking, until his father retrieved his oxygen tank, backed the rig out of the drive, and headed off toward town. When the rig went out of view, he went to the phone and dialed Clive's number.

The phone rang and rang until the answering machine picked up. Creed figured Clive to be in the bed, sleeping off the all-nighter they'd pulled.

"Clive, pick up the damn phone!" Creed yelled into the answering machine. "PICK UP, DAMMIT!"

Chapter 13

Burdy had not been able to attend the funeral for Hunk and Mary Nelle Kincer or Watson Loxley. She was still in the hospital when they put those three in the ground and covered them with dirt and the prayers of loved ones grieving. She'd been home a couple of weeks now but still wasn't able to sleep much on account of every time she shut her eyes, she seen that gunman, heard the cries of Mary Nelle and poor young Watson Loxley begging for their lives. Neither she nor Hunk had cried out at all. Maybe it was the stoic in them. Why give any gunman that kind of power? Burdy wasn't the cowering type. She did as she was told, but there was no way she was going to beg some deranged stranger for her life.

It's not that she was ready to meet her maker so much as that she refused to give the gunman the satisfaction of fear. She took the Apostle Paul at his word when he said, "For me, to live is Christ, to die is gain." Burdy figured Hunk probably had a similar approach. Truth was, when a man holds a gun to your head and tells you he's going to kill you, he's either going to do what he says or not, and no amount of carrying on is going to change the outcome. More than likely, getting all up in a gunman's face is only going to piss him off further and hasten one's demise. Burdy didn't know if the reason the gunman let her live was because she didn't say two words to him, didn't even look at him directly, but she figured it was as good a reason as any she could think of.

Still, the fact that she—the oldest person in Laidlow's that day—was allowed to live, while the gunman killed that poor Loxley boy, him only nineteen, was disturbing her something fierce. For the first time in her life really, Burdy felt some sense of the guilt that Zeb had experienced. While she hadn't been the one to pull the trigger, the way Zeb had, she felt the weight of the death of that young man with every moment. She could not allow herself to be happy that she survived for the recognition that others had not. The natural order of things mandated that the oldest die long before the youngest. Burdy had defied the natural order, and instead of making her feel lucky, it simply made her feel like some great injustice had occurred and it was mostly her own fault.

Burdy's Aunty Tay always said that guilt is a smothering thing. She used to wonder what Aunty Tay meant by that, but no longer. Burdy come to think it was like having a caul over one's head all the time. It was hard for her to think clearly. Wheedin had been afraid to leave her momma at the house alone because Burdy hadn't seemed herself since the shooting. But Burdy knew what Wheedin didn't yet know—she would never again be the woman she had been before. When a gunman holds a loaded weapon up to your head and screams obscenities into your ear, it changes you in ways you can't begin to describe. It takes a long time to feel normal again, and even then the normal you feel ain't the same normal you used to feel. It's something altogether different.

That's the kind of thing Burdy tried to explain to Detective Wiley when he come by the house about a week and half after she returned home. Wheedin, who had been hovering over her momma like a nesting mockingbird, ran into town to pick up some things at the grocer's while Burdy and Detective Wiley sat at the kitchen table, him with a notepad, Burdy with a pebble in her hand.

"That's a nice stone," Wiley said. "Mind if I see it?" Burdy handed him the polished stone. "What is it?"

"Rose quartz," Burdy replied. "I keep a jarful of them over there." She pointed to the shelf where she kept some of healing roots. "Some call them worry stones."

"Worry stones?" Wiley rubbed the stone with his thumb. It was smooth to the touch, soothing to turn over.

"Yeah. They's supposed to help a person with their worries. I used to have a prayer stone I used, but when it got gone, I took to using these here worry stones." Burdy took another one from her apron pocket.

"What happened to your prayer stone?" Wiley asked, handing back the well-worn pebble.

"I give it away to somebody who needed it more than me," Burdy said. "My Auntie Tay always said that rose quartz could cure the brokenhearted and the wounded in spirit."

"Is that so?"

"Well, that's what Tay said. I ain't so sure anymore."

"Why's that?" Wiley removed a notebook and a pen from his shirt pocket.

"It don't seem to be helping me all that much," Burdy replied. "Can I get you a glass of iced tea?"

"No, thank you."

"How about a glass of water?"

"I appreciate the offer, but I'm good." Wiley took note of the walker parked beside the table where Burdy was sitting. He wasn't surprised that she still needed it to get around. The gunshot wound had been substantial. She was lucky she hadn't lost her entire leg, or so Wheedin had told him.

Burdy seen him looking at the walker. "I'll give you a buffalo nickel if you will take that thing with you when you leave."

Wiley laughed. It had been a long time since anybody had offered him a buffalo nickel. He was tempted to take Burdy up on her offer. "Do you need it still?"

"I suppose I do. I haven't got the strength in my leg that I used to have. Doctor tells me I might not never again walk without that thing. I'm aiming to prove him wrong." Burdy pulled the lame leg around. "It ain't healed long enough for the scar to form, but when it does, I'll show it to you, if you like."

"That's quite alright," Wiley replied. Wounds, healing or otherwise, made him downright nauseated. Wiley couldn't handle a trip to the dentist to get his teeth cleaned, much less an open wound of any kind. His weakness gave his fellow officers much-needed comic relief. They loved harassing him about it. Wiley protested that if he had liked hospitals and wounds, he would have become a surgeon, not a detective.

Burdy put the stones back in her apron.

"So those stones, they aren't helping you. Is it because of the shooting?" Wiley studied Burdy as she sat silent for a good while. Even though it was October and she had lost a lot of blood in the shooting, Burdy's Melungeon skin had retained the brown of summer. Her white hair, pulled back at the nape, braided and twisted into a bun, gave her an ethereal look. Sitting at the kitchen table with a glint of the morning sun casting a luminous glow behind her, Burdy looked regal, like some mother goddess of a long-forgotten tribe.

"Yes, it's because of the shooting," she said softly. "Every time I close my eyes, it all comes back to me. All of it."

"What? What comes back to you?"

"The yelling. The cursing. The gunfire. The crying. The gunfire. The pleading. The gunfire. The blood. The gunfire. The dying."

Detective Wiley was taking notes, scribbling as much of what Burdy was saying as he could manage.

"The dying," she repeated.

"What about the gunman? What do you remember about him?"

"He was hysterical," Burdy said. "That's what I remember."

"What do you mean by hysterical?"

"Like a madman. Like an angry madman."

"Can you be more specific?"

Burdy shifted in her chair, leaned forward, picked at a yellow thread come loose from the embroidery Maizee had sewn into the tablecloth years prior. "It's difficult to explain. When somebody kills another person, can they ever be in their right mind? But he surely wasn't in his. He was waving that gun, screaming curse words every other second, telling us to lie facedown in the vitamin and aspirin aisle."

"Did you get a good look at him?"

"No."

"So the shooter wasn't anybody you recognized at all?"

"No. I don't go up to Bean Station much. I know a few people up around that area but not many. Some of them folks worked over at Pressmen's when I was there. I knowed Dukey and Jane Laidlow when they owned the place, but I didn't know the new owners well, other than their names. 'Course, I knew the Loxley boy killed."

Burdy quit pulling on the thread, put her hands in her lap. Her shoulders slumped. "Let me ask you a question, Detective Wiley."

"Sure," Wiley said. He put his pen flat across his notebook.

"How come that gunman didn't kill me and killed that young boy instead? I'm old. But that boy had his whole life ahead of him."

Wiley hated these moments, the ones where some tragedy left the survivors dealing with guilt. He'd come across it many times throughout his career. The worst was when a woman over at Morristown backed a van out of the driveway and killed her own three-year-old daughter, who had run out the front door to give her momma a kiss good-bye. The grandmother had chased after the little girl, had screamed from the porch as the child ran behind the vehicle, screamed for her daughter to stop, not back up any further, but it all happened so quickly, as most tragedies do.

That mother turned to drinking as a way to suppress the memory of killing her child, and the grandmother got early-onset dementia within a year's time of the accident. There was no question that the dementia was brought on by the death of that poor baby. Three lives were ruined that day, not to mention the dad and then the surviving brother, who turned out to be a fine boy, trying to make up for all the wrongs done the family.

"I don't know, Mrs. Luttrell. I wish I had a better answer for you than that, but I don't. There is a certain randomness to life that I simply can't understand or explain. All I know is that those who died wouldn't want you to feel bad about surviving. They'd want you to accept life as the gift it is and do your best to make it count."

"I thought I was making my life count before all this happened."

"I am sure you were." There were no words of comfort to offer someone dealing with the guilt of living. Wiley knew that. Still, he felt compelled to try and offer Burdy a different perspective than the warped one she was noodling over. "Surviving is neither a punishment nor a reward."

"What do you mean?" Burdy said. "A punishment or a reward?"

"Maybe I'm not saying it right," Wiley replied. "I just mean that I don't think God let those other people die because they did something wrong and you live because you did something right. Or because He was finished with them and not yet finished with you. I think we all die as incomplete works of God, whether we die at nineteen or ninety-nine."

"Maybe so," Burdy said. She didn't feel much different on the inside at eighty than she did at eighteen, that's for sure. If anything, she valued each day more than she did when she was younger and had a lifetime spanning out before her.

It was that recognition, though, that made her wince whenever she thought of the Loxley boy and all the life he would miss out on, life that Burdy had already gotten to live—falling in love, having a child, purposeful work. Watson Loxley would never experience any of that. The very thought of it made her heart ache.

Wiley noticed a weariness come upon Mrs. Luttrell. He knew it as a sign of depression common to those who lived through horrors untold. His first inclination was to stop the interview and come back another day. But Wiley knew that the longer he put off talking with Mrs. Luttrell, the further behind the investigation would get. And it had already been going on long enough.

Chief Conley was taking heat from the community for not making an arrest yet, and it weren't but a few weeks out from the shooting. Wiley knew the public didn't have a clue what all went into a murder investigation. People watched too many of those criminal shows on television and figured (wrongly) that they could solve a murder in a day or two. They figured (again wrongly) that any investigation that took more than two days, much less months, to solve was simply the result of police bungling.

Lord, it was hard being a cop sometimes. Some days Wiley wished he'd left the mountains of Tennessee for the waters of Mobile Bay. He had an uncle who lived on a thirty-foot sailboat parked in a marina outside Fairhope, Alabama. Wiley's uncle made his money through day trading. Wiley wasn't too sure what day traders did, but whatever it was, his uncle must have been pretty good at it because he didn't work regular like other folks. He came and went as he pleased and never seemed to have want of much. Granted, his uncle never married, never had a family, but he never had the obligations those required, either.

Wiley looked at his watch. He was due to meet his wife at the therapist's office later. They had been going through a rough spot, not their first. If they could manage it, they'd celebrate their twentieth anniversary in December. Wiley wasn't sure they'd make it, though. He was having a difficult time forgiving Marly for having an affair with a city councilman, but he was trying for their daughter's sake.

"I know you must be worn out, Mrs. Luttrell," Wiley said. "I promise not to keep you much longer, if you could just answer a couple more questions for me."

"I am tired," Burdy acknowledged. All that muster she used to be able to work up was long gone. Burdy took to her bed a lot these days, and when she wasn't in bed, she took to the recliner in the living room.

Wiley picked up his pen again. "Is there anything else you can remember about that day? Anything at all about the shooter?"

"Other than his hateful voice, very little."

"Do you think if you heard it again, you'd recognize it?"

"I don't think I could forget it if I tried." Burdy reached for her walker. "I hate to be rude, Detective Wiley, but I didn't sleep well last night. I am worn out."

Wiley stood. "Of course." He handed Burdy a card with his phone number. "If you think of anything else, please don't hesitate to call me."

Burdy took the card and put it in her pocket. She shuffled ahead of the officer as she led him through the living room. Opening the front door, Burdy started to say good-bye when something came to her. "There is something. I hadn't remembered it until just this minute."

Wiley stopped halfway out the door, one foot on either side of the doorsill. He didn't want to press Burdy for fear that whatever she remembered would just as quickly be forgotten.

"Well, I don't know if it actually happened or if it's something I dreamed of afterwards." Burdy looked at the palms of her stubby hands, as if searching for direction in the lines.

"Even if it was something you dreamed, it might be of help to us," Wiley said. "Sometimes our subconscious does the work in our sleep that our conscious is unable to do when we're awake."

"It was something Hunk said right before the shooter killed him."

Wiley waited. A bright red cardinal flew out of the chokeberry bush next to the house. Its duller mate followed close behind. "Yes?" he said, expectantly.

"He said, 'Son, don't do this. It'll kill your daddy.'"

Wiley wrote down exactly what Burdy said, word for word, in that pocket notebook of his. "He called the shooter, 'Son'? You sure that's what you heard?"

"I done told you I'm not sure if I heard it or if I dreamed it," Burdy replied. She was clearly agitated. "But that's what I just now recalled."

"Okay, thank you. Please call me if anything else comes to you. Anything."

"Yes, yes," Burdy said. "I have your number right here." She patted her apron pocket and shut the door between them as Wiley bounded down the porch steps and practically did a hop-skip to his car. Finally, he thought he had something to go on. He wasn't sure what any of it meant, but he was sure that whether Mrs. Luttrell dreamed it or not, Hunk's last words held a truth about the identity of the shooter.

Chapter 14

Burdy felt no urge to call Detective Wiley after he left. And he wasn't the only person she was avoiding speaking with. Burdy had come home from the hospital with every intention of getting in touch with Clint. He needed to know why she had missed his calls. But then she got home, and the thought of telling Clint over the phone what happened seemed more daunting than she'd imagined. How does one go about calling one's lover and announcing, "Oh, by the way, sorry I missed your calls. I've been hospitalized after a gunman shot me and killed three others."

Burdy did not think she could handle it if Clint responded the way almost everyone did, by telling her how lucky she was that she wasn't killed. Luck had nothing to do with what happened at the Bean Station pharmacy that day. The lucky people were the ones who stayed away from the pharmacy, the ones who weren't having to live with the nightmare of figuring out how come they survived while others died.

Wheedin had stayed by her mother's side throughout the hospital ordeal. The only way the surgeon could save Burdy's leg was by rebuilding it, so she came home with a steel rod in her upper thigh to help stabilize the leg that the gunman had destroyed. Wheedin had never been much of a caretaker before—she'd never needed to be—but now Burdy needed help with the most basic daily needs.

Early on, Wheedin had to change out Burdy's dressing twice a day. Those first few days, Leela and Doc came by and helped Wheedin do it, until she figured out the best possible method of wrapping her momma's leg with one arm (she tucked the extra bandage wrap underneath her chin, sometimes in her teeth, as she carefully twisted it around her momma's leg). Burdy hated being on the receiving end of caregiving. Hated it in every possible way, but having dealt with more than her share of recalcitrant patients, she decided that she would be as cooperative as her independent nature would allow, which, granted, wasn't much.

She started each day with good intentions, thanking Wheedin for the gravy and biscuits or the grits and bacon served each morning at 7:30 a.m., and she thanked her again at 12:30 p.m. when Wheedin served a lunch of pork chops and lima beans or pimento cheese sandwiches and fried peach pies. The church folks brought in supper every night for the first three weeks, so at least Wheedin didn't have to worry about cooking for her momma three times.

It embarrassed them both when Wheedin had to help Burdy with her bathroom duties. Burdy could get to the bathroom but she needed help with the toilet. She couldn't lower herself or raise herself up without help those first ten days or so. Then there was the matter of bathing. Wheedin had to give her momma a sponge bath—or, as Burdy referred to it, "a whore's bath"—because the leg wound could not be immersed in water. Washing her mother's backside and privates was something that Wheedin never imagined she'd have to do. But Wheedin bathed her mother nearly every day for three weeks with a wash cloth from a tin basin, and she did it with great gentleness and respect.

"How do you like bathing your big baby?" Burdy had teased, hoping to lighten the discomfort of the moment. She had long desired a more intimate relationship with her daughter, but this wasn't what she had in mind.

"I like it fine," Wheedin replied. After patting her dry, Wheedin would rub a lotion made of rosemary and lavender over her momma's rough feet and elbows, down her arms and legs, and over the back of her neck and shoulders. That rubdown was Burdy's favorite part of the day. She loved the smell of the natural herbs and of being tended to in such a tender way by her own daughter.

"I never thought you would be the one taking care of me," Burdy said.

"That's makes two of us," Wheedin replied. She winked at her momma to let her know she was just teasing her.

Most days passed along in a routine of meals and baths and dressing changes, along with trips to the physical therapist or the surgeon to follow up on the progression of healing. Every now and again, Wheedin would be short-tempered with Burdy or vice versa, but for the most part, the two women worked in a quiet synchronicity, doing what needed to be done without much complaint, despite the fact that neither woman wanted to be in the position they found themselves. Even so, it had been the way of the women in their family for ages. Maybe it was that way with all women throughout all ages, this changing of the guard in the caretaking routine.

Burdy had thought Rain would come see her when she got home, but he hadn't, not yet. Whenever she asked Doc or Leela about Rain and why he still hadn't been by the house, they made up excuses for him. Leela would recount all the reasons why it was best Rain hadn't come around, but Burdy, never one to lie to herself, saw right through all that. She knew the real truth was that Rain was avoiding her. He didn't want to talk about what he'd found in Burdy's bottom dresser drawer. Not right now, anyway.

The letters were gone. The blue velvet box was still there, wrapped up and hidden in the middle of her drawer. Burdy went looking for it in early October, when her leg had healed up enough that she could get around a bit by herself. She waited until a Sunday when Wheedin was off at church, so she wouldn't be bothered. Using her walker and an embroidered footstool that had sat at the end of her bed for ages without any use whatsoever, Burdy lowered herself down, her bum leg straight out to one side, so she could reach that drawer. When she pulled out the velvet box, she thought that perhaps Rain had never found the letters, had never even gone in search of them. But when she opened it and discovered that all those yellowed letters from Zeb were missing, she knew Rain had taken them.

In a way it was a relief. Secrets grow heavier with age. The older one gets, the harder it is to bear such heavy things alone. Burdy had never meant to keep Zeb a secret from Rain. She had always intended to tell him about his father when the time was right. But maybe she had lied to herself over that; maybe she wasn't as honest as she portrayed herself to be. Can a person be honest as daylight and yet keep certain things stashed away in the darkness? Especially something as important as Zeb being alive and not dead, as everyone in the Bend had always assumed?

Burdy didn't blame Rain for being upset with her. She was upset with herself over the mess she'd created. That was part of the reason she didn't want to speak to Clint, the reason she hadn't called him when she came home or picked up the phone when he called for her. She needed to set things right between her and Rain first.

But how? That was the question nagging at Burdy as she replaced the blue velvet box in its hidden spot and, with the help of her walker, raised herself back up. Pushing herself over to the window, Burdy looked out to the hills beyond Ida Mosely's fields. The trees sparkled like rubies and topaz in the mid-morning light. In a whisper, Burdy recited a favorite psalm that Auntie Tay had taught her long ago:

I lift my eyes to the mountains,
where does my help come from?
My help comes from the Lord,
the Maker of heaven and earth.
He will not let your foot slip,
he who watches over you will not slumber;
indeed, he who watches over Israel
will neither slumber or sleep.

89

The Lord watches over you,
the Lord is your shade at your right hand;
 the sun will not harm you by day
nor the moon by night.
The Lord will keep you from all harm,
he will watch over your life.
The Lord will watch over your coming and going
Both now and forevermore.

Auntie Tay used to pray this psalm over Burdy and her cousin Hota every night as she tucked them into bed. At the time, Burdy had considered it nothing more than a sweet evening ritual, like when Tay put sprigs of bay leaves under their pillows to ward off nightmares and invite sweet dreams.

After Burdy married and had a child of her own, a child over whom she prayed the same psalm, she considered the scriptures more thoughtfully, as a promise as well as a prayer. Motherhood was inherent with worry, and after Tibbis died, Burdy needed all the guidance she could tap into. One of the problems with being a strong woman is determining who to run to when you are afraid and doubt yourself. Burdy determined early on that she would turn to Creator God, primarily because of the prayer Tay prayed over her all those years earlier.

But now, even as she stood before the window, repeating the words aloud, Burdy questioned the validity of that psalm. While it appeared to others that the Lord had kept Burdy out of harm's way, that He had watched out for all her comings and goings, it sure didn't feel that way to her. And what about Watson Loxley? How come God didn't keep that young boy and Hunk and Mary Nelle Kincer out of harm's way? Why didn't God have that shooter trip on his way into the pharmacy and kill himself instead? Better yet, why didn't God just seize him up with a major heart attack that morning? Save them all some heartache in the process?

Con Christian passed the house, talking to himself as Burdy looked on. People at the Bend believed Con was endowed with special powers. They believed that in part because Con was always saying it. Still, given her own healer's gift, Burdy believed that God had picked Con out to be some sort of mountain harbinger. He had come up to her place the week before the shooting and stood in the middle of the street calling her name. When she'd come around the house to see what all the fuss was about, he said, "I have a message for you, Widow Luttrell."

It had been a long time since anyone had called her the Widow Luttrell to her face. It annoyed Burdy but she let it pass, figuring she'd let Con have his say and then she'd get back to her chores in the garden.

"I'm listening with all my ears," she replied.

Then Con issued his warning: "Do not be afraid of the terror by night or the arrow that flies by day. A thousand may fall at your side, and ten thousand at your right hand, but it shall not approach you."

The first part of the warning was something Burdy was already familiar with. It was one of the final things Tibbis said to Burdy the last time she took some smokes and beautyberries up to his gravehouse. She'd retorted that he should have taken his own advice, given that shitepoke kid from over at Johnson City had killed him with an arrow. But the second part of Con's message had meant nothing to Burdy. Nothing at all.

Standing at the window, watching Con Christian trudge up the road, Burdy couldn't help but wish she'd paid attention to his earlier warning about a thousand people falling at her side. It didn't matter if it was one person or tens of thousands of people, when you are the one who lives through the slaughter, you can't help but feel that God has made a mistake.

The one person Burdy wished she could talk to more than any other wasn't Clint—it was Zeb. Who better than Zeb could understand the mixed emotions of gratefulness and guilt Burdy was experiencing?

Chapter 15

Rain put Zeb's letters in a backpack and hiked up to Horseshoe Falls. It was mid-October and bursts of yellow witch hazel nudged up against the trail, obscuring it in some places. Along with the letters, he'd packed a sleeping bag and a few camping necessities—flashlight, matches, beef jerky, water, a Colt .45, and a half-bottle of whiskey. He'd drunk the other half yesterday, even though he'd woken up in his mother's house promising himself he wouldn't.

Drinking to excess was not something that generally appealed to Rain. He'd have a glass of good wine on occasion, sometimes a glass of bourbon in the evening or a swallow of shine whenever he was back in the Bend, but never much more than that. Prior to finding those letters from his father, Rain had gone his entire life without getting drunk. He could never understand the people who said that drinking helped them relax. Rain didn't find it relaxing to be out of control of his body. Until recently, he had never experienced the anesthetic effect of drinking. That effect appealed to him now.

Burdy had watched him leave. He saw her watching from behind the screen door on the back porch. At any other time, he would have gone over and been part of the welcoming party when she came home. He would have made sure her leaves were raked and her porches swept. He would have put pumpkins on the front steps and laughed with Doc over the jack-o-lantern story his momma Maizee used to beg Doc to repeat. A story that Doc did repeat to Rain every October throughout his childhood.

But now, every time he thought of how Burdy kept the knowledge of his father to herself all these years, Rain's stomach burned. How had she managed to do that even in the wake of his mother's death? Rain trudged up the hillside at a pace faster than normal, fueled by the sheer anger he felt toward the woman he'd always loved with abandon, whom he had believed loved him the same way.

What a week it had been. Rain had woken to the news that markets worldwide had crashed. The Dow Jones fell by 508 points by closing on Monday. President Reagan called a press conference to try and reassure panicked Americans. He referred to the crash as "a long overdue correction" and called for Americans to respond with calm. Every president faced with a stock market crash—or, as Reagan preferred, "an overdue correction"—likely tells Americans to keep calm and continue spending, Rain thought as he drank coffee at Leela and Doc's that morning, listening along with them to the president's remarks.

Doc and Leela grew up on the heels of the Great Depression caused by the crash of 1929.

"Why do these market crashes always happen in October?" Rain had asked.

"I don't know," Doc replied. He hit the mute button on the remote, drowning out a question from United Press correspondent Helen Thomas. "But one of my dad's brothers jumped from a building in New York City when that first crash happened."

"You never told me that," Leela-Ma said. She tucked her feet underneath her on the couch and covered them with a blue-and-white afghan.

"Never had reason to, I suppose," Doc said. "I don't know much more about it than that. He worked for some bank. Didn't have much to do with the family back home. He married some hifalutin woman from New York City, so he was buried up there. I never knew him. I was just a kid when that market crashed. It didn't have much effect on us no-how, given we was already so poor we didn't have a pot to piss in or a window to throw it out of."

Rain and Leela had laughed at Doc's remark even though they both knew there was much truth in it.

This new crash would have a broader impact now that people in the Bend were working in towns and investing in savings and retirement. It also meant trouble for Rain. Part of his job required fundraising for programs to benefit the disabled. Rain knew that whoever Ellis had temporarily put in charge of his job would face an even bigger challenge now to meet the year-end goals, not to mention all the monies lost due to the drop in the Dow Jones. Typically, the months between October and December were their most successful, but when people panic the first thing they do is quit giving to the causes they've long supported. Rain contacted Ellis to see if he should come back to Rhode Island, but Ellis reassured him all would be okay, no need to rush back just yet.

Monday's events sobered Rain up a bit, made him realize that if he wanted to know what happened to his father, he was going to have to read those letters, sooner rather than later. He couldn't think of a more fitting place to do that than up at Horseshoe Falls. It was quiet, and there would be no one around to interrupt him. He'd always felt closer to his parents up there than anywhere else in the world.

He rose before daybreak on Wednesday, slipped on his jeans and an old flannel shirt still hanging in his mother's closet. Nobody had ever bothered packing up the house. Burdy had left it as it was the day Maizee died. Doc and Leela had come by later and taken Rain's things, a few of Maizee's things, but it was as if by not changing anything, they could hold fast to all that they had lost when Maizee and Zeb died.

Only Zeb hadn't died, Rain reminded himself as he fastened the last button on his father's old work shirt. It was just that nobody but him and Burdy knew the truth. For all Doc and Leela-Ma or anybody else in the Bend knew, Zebulon Hurd died a war hero fighting the Germans on the beaches of Normandy.

And Rain only knew part of the truth, just that Zeb had lived and, for whatever reason, had chosen not to return home, to abandon his ailing wife and his disabled son. Rain didn't even know if Zeb was still alive. Only Burdy knew that, and Rain wasn't about to walk over to her place and ask her anything, particularly not anything about the father who hadn't thought enough of his young child to come home and care for him.

Rain wasn't a father himself, a fact that bothered him although he never let on to others. Still, had he become a father, Rain could not imagine anything—other than death—that would keep him away from his child.

He pushed aside a branch and bent over to pick up a granola wrapper from the trail. Rain couldn't understand the laziness and carelessness of some people. He'd read disturbing stories about the trash some mountain climbers leave behind on Mt. Everest and the junk visitors to Yellowstone throw into the geysers. He'd even read one National Geographic story about how Morning Glory, one of the geysers, spit back out socks, towels, handkerchiefs, and a couple hundred dollars in nickels, dimes, and pennies.

Fortunately, most people in the Bend were respectful of the land. When a person makes a living from the land, as the people in the Bend always had, they're keenly aware of the mutual yet perilous relationship between man and nature. Burdy had taught Rain that. She'd also taught him the names of roots and the healing powers of certain plants and berries. Rain wasn't sure he could do it anymore, but there had been a time in his youth when he knew he could live in the woods, feasting on bugs and wild honey and berries the way John the Baptist had.

His time in Rhode Island had taken him away from the land of his youth. The connection he'd once nurtured was long gone. Now he could hardly tell the difference between a pawpaw and a ginseng. After his first year in Rhode Island, Rain's long-time girlfriend, Mary Esther Newton, had accused him of becoming "too Yankeefied." During his second year there, Kade told Rain that Mary Esther had up and married some fellow from Bennettsville, South Carolina.

Rain stopped to take a drink of water from his canteen. He could see Tibbis's gravehouse from the rock where he stood. One of Burdy's walking sticks was leaning up against it. Hard to know if she left it by accident or on purpose. When he first fell in love with Mary Esther, Rain thought the two of them would grow a great love like the one shared between Burdy and Tibbis. Or his own parents.

They'd met in high school. Mary Esther's father was the math teacher at the Tennessee School for the Deaf. Mary Esther went to a school for hearing kids, but she'd often hang out in her daddy's class after school, waiting for him to finish up for the day. They lived in a two-story house on the edge of town. Mary Esther, at fifteen, wasn't old enough to drive yet; and she was loathe to ride the school bus all the way home, so she'd walk the three blocks east from her school to the deaf school.

She was named after both of her grandmothers, but she looked most like her Mamaw Esther, who had been a champion swimmer at Auburn. Mary Esther was slim-hipped, small-breasted, and button-nosed. She possessed a well-scrubbed tomboy look. When she got flustered—something that didn't happen all that much—her neck and cheeks flamed red. Her gold hair was thick and straight, except for right around the temples, where it had a tendency to kink up, a trait that Rain often teased her about.

Unlike other hearing kids, Mary Esther knew how to sign. She had her family history to thank for that. Her father had grown up the hearing child of deaf parents. Mary Esther learned to sign so she could communicate with her grandparents.

Their first date was her idea. She asked Rain to walk with her over to Feagin's Burger Shack, where they shared a plate of curly fries and talked, mostly about UT basketball. Mary Esther played forward for her high school team—the Knights—and was hoping to bankroll those talents into a scholarship to UT.

That first date led to another and another and another. For the next four years, Rain and Mary Esther were inseparable. College finally split them up. Mary Esther got the scholarship she so badly wanted, while Rain headed north to Gallaudet. The separation proved too much. Mary Esther never wanted to live anywhere but Tennessee. She wanted to have a family and to teach high school like her daddy. Rain had bigger dreams than that. Or so it had seemed all those years ago.

He lost track of Mary Esther and then heard from Kade that she'd married and lived in a fine house near Sewanee, where her husband was a professor. At Gallaudet, Rain had dated quite a bit. A couple of the women would have made good life-long partners, but the timing never seemed to work. Rain was focused on building a career. He had something to prove to himself, if to no one else. He needed to assure himself that his limited deafness wasn't a handicap but a gift.

The hearing loss made him much more aware of the world he inhabited. Rain paid attention to things most people missed, like how fast a speaker's lips moved, the arch of an eyebrow, the nervous twitch of a nose rub. These seemingly minor things communicated in ways that words alone never could. Rain became skillful at reading the hidden ticks of body language. In fact, he'd started doing workshops on the subject that were often filled to capacity, and every summer he taught a handful of Special Forces operatives how to decipher these telling ticks of human movement.

Rain felt the thunder of Horseshoe Falls long before he reached the waterfall. He felt it first in the pads of his feet, then his heels, and then it was as if his entire calves were trembling in response to the waters rushing off the cliff top.

Whatever memory Rain had of the great-grandfather chestnut that towered at the top of the falls came more from the stories told him by Burdy, Leela-Ma, and Doc than from his own recollection. The tree had finally fallen victim to blight and, like all the ancestral chestnuts of the region, succumbed to a disfiguring and withering death.

Rain glanced around, scouting for a good spot to set up camp for the night. He settled on a dry patch of land between two trees, a good distance back from the waterfall. He didn't want the letters or anything else he brought with him getting wet. Sunset wasn't far off, and the air, which had been unseasonably warm for mid-October, turned crisp.

He unrolled his sleeping bag and stretched out beneath a canopy of golden branches, trying to remember the last time he'd spent the night in the woods. The best he could recollect, it was that first September after his graduation from Gallaudet. He and Kade spent a week hiking through North Georgia and Tennessee. It was just the sort of transition period Rain had needed before heading off to start his career, a career that would carry him far away from all things familiar.

They were sitting atop Clingman's Dome one afternoon, late, waiting on the sun to bed down, when Kade began to tell Rain the stories of Maizee. Rain's own memories of his mother were sparse. He recalled how her black hair brushed against his cheek whenever she bent over to kiss him, and the confusion he'd felt the night she'd enlisted his help in killing monster bugs only she could see. At first, young Rain had thought they were playing a game, but Maizee wasn't laughing; if he remembered rightly, she was weeping. And he remembered their last walk to Leela-Ma's, something they had done hundreds of times together. Him holding his momma's hand, her carrying him when his little legs failed to keep up with her stride. But Rain's memory of his momma ended with a felt storyboard, the one Doc had used to help explain to the young deaf boy that his mother and father had gone to be with Jesus.

Those stories Kade shared atop Clingman's Dome as the sun settled in a reddening fury were the ones that enabled Rain to know his momma more fully.

"I kissed her once," Kade had said.

Rain had pointed at Kade, indicating the universal sign for "You?" and registering his surprise.

"Yeah, me." Kade laughed. "We were on a hay ride along with Wheedin and your daddy. Only he wasn't your daddy yet. He was driving. I was in the back with Wheedin and your momma. I knew she didn't really like me but I was brash, full of myself. I grabbed her when she wasn't expecting it and kissed her. I might have slipped her the tongue if she hadn't hauled off and slapped me."

Rain threw his head back in laughter. He'd never thought about the men who might have been attracted to his momma before, never imagined her as a teenager, or a girl. He wasn't surprised that Kade had put the moves on Maizee. A handful of family photographs, yellowing with age, had preserved her beauty. Even as a boy, Rain recognized that his momma possessed an uncommon loveliness. It made him miss the mother he barely knew all the more.

"Oh, Lord, your mother was full of piss and vinegar, and a spirit that soared far above all these mountains," Kade told him. He opened his arms wide, taking in the expanse before them. "I was a tad bit jealous, although not surprised, when I learned your daddy and momma got hitched. And when you came along, well, I don't believe I have ever seen two people more smitten. I doubt any child has been more loved than you, Rain. How I wish you could have known that love throughout your life. They'd be so proud of the man you've become. I'm sure proud of you."

Listening to Kade, Rain squinted at the last of the sunset's fire and didn't bother to swipe away the tears falling from his cheeks. Kade knew better than anyone how much Rain had missed by not having Maizee and Zeb around to raise him up.

"After your daddy went away, this was your momma's favorite time of day," Kade remarked. "I think she found an odd comfort in the in-between hour."

"Doc always called it the gloaming hour," Rain said. "That time when the darkness hasn't come yet, but the light is waning."

"That reminds me of a song your momma used to sing. She often sang it while sitting on the porch, rocking you to sleep for the night. Do you remember it?"

Rain shook his head. He had no memory of his momma rocking him or singing to him.

Kade picked up the guitar he'd brought along. In those days, Kade didn't go anywhere without his guitar. He began to strum and hum the tune. "Any of it coming back to you? It's called In the Gloaming. It was written long ago by the English poet, Meta Orred, I believe."

"No," Rain said. He could only hear bits and pieces. "Sing louder."

Turning so he faced Rain, Kade plucked out and sang the tune that had been one of Maizee's favorites, a song she'd turned into a lullaby for Rain:

In the gloaming, oh, my darling!
When the lights are dim and low,
And the quiet shadows falling,
Softly come and softly go;

When the winds are sobbing faintly
With a gentle unknown woe,
Will you think of me, and love me,
As you did once long ago?

In the gloaming, oh, my darling!
Think not bitterly of me!

Tho' I passed away in silence
Left you lonely, set you free;

For my heart was crush'd with longing,
What had been could never be;
It was best to leave you thus, dear,
Best for you, and best for me.

Now, on his solo camping trip, Rain could almost hear Kade's voice ringing out and bouncing off the hills. Suddenly, a boulder fell from atop Horseshoe Falls into the pool below, creating a splash that startled Rain and broke his reverie. He jumped up and spotted two men at the top of the ridge. The bigger of the two had his hands around the throat of a long-haired fellow. They were yelling and fighting perilously close to the edge of the Falls. Rain feared one of the men was about to end up dead. He didn't know whether to run toward them or to back up and hide behind one of the trees for worry of being involved in something he wanted no part of.

He ran toward the trail to the top but only got a few steps when he heard screaming. He looked up and saw the blond fella fall, tumbling, scrambling, trying desperately to turn himself, save himself, twisting for the blue pool below and not the rocks. It was only moments before he hit the pool that Rain recognized him.

"Creed!" he yelled. "CREED!"

Rain's yelling startled the man on the ledge, who eased himself away.

Chapter 16

Pam and Larry headed home after the dinner date, leaving Kade and Thomasina on their own. As they walked away, Pam elbowed Larry, who remarked that she might have done a good thing, setting those two up.

Not ready to say good night, Kade offered to show Thomasina the Knoxville she knew nothing about. He drove her around town first, pointing to one Civil War landmark after another. The story that resonated was the one about the Mabry-Hazen home up on Dandridge. Thomasina remembered it because of the stories about the granddaughters of Joseph Mabry. One sister died of an eating disorder after her husband drank himself to death, and the younger sister became a recluse after she sued her lover for failing to marry her. Seems she had to admit before God and everybody that they'd had relations prior to marriage, so nobody in Knoxville society wanted anything to do with her after that very public admission.

As he told the stories, Kade laughed at the melodrama of these women's lives, but Thomasina felt sorry for them.

"Women in those days were pitifully trapped by the conventions of their culture," she said. "They were expected to marry, have babies, cook, and clean, and woe to the woman who didn't marry, who had other dreams for her life."

"I suppose so," Kade said, immediately regretful. "I still see that sort of thing every day in my line of work."

"You do?" Thomasina replied. "How so?"

"I encounter men who barter their women, their sons and daughters, even their toddler children for drugs, for the next high. Whatever moral center they once possessed is long gone. I had a call just last week about a fellow who had caged his girlfriend's six-year-old son, starved him until he was only twenty-five pounds, and was offering up his girlfriend's four-year-old daughter to whoever would pay him $250 for an hour to have sex with the child. How is she ever going to recover?"

Thomasina shook her head. "I don't know. I really don't know." She'd worked the emergency room, had seen children come in with unexplained bruises and broken bones. She knew Kade spoke the truth.

"I saw that once with a six-month-old," she said. "Only it wasn't her mother's live-in who traded the baby for sex. It was the mother. It was a long time ago—the girl would be thirteen or fourteen now—but I still think of her and how she will manage to navigate life in any healthy way at all."

"It's hard. I know." Kade sighed. "You can't ever get the faces of those children out of your head. And these women, no matter what, they will not leave their men. I don't understand that."

"I do," Thomasina said.

Kade turned to look at her, nearly running through a four-way stop. "Seriously? Thomasina nodded, then turned away from Kade. Damn addicts and their foul addictions. They've just about ruined mountain life. When I was growing up, nobody even locked their doors. We would run around outside all day long. I used to fish down on the Holston from sunup to sundown. My mother didn't worry about where I was. She knew she could find me on the riverbank. Neighbors were the people we trusted when kin wasn't available. Now they're the people we hide from, lest they turn out to be an addict."

"Not everyone who abuses women and children are addicts," she said. "My husband was an attorney."

"Your husband abused you?" Kade pulled to the side of the road. They were headed up to Sharp's Ridge. He wanted to show Thomasina the lights of the city from above, but the conversation had turned much heavier than he'd expected. He left the truck running but shoved the gear into park. "I'm sorry." Carefully, he reached for Thomasina's hand.

"That's why I left Baltimore," she said, allowing him to take her hand. "Sometimes it's harder to speak up when your husband has money and power and can discredit everything you say." Thomasina couldn't look at Kade. She stared at the floorboard. "Even now, I'm ashamed to tell you about it."

"Ashamed? Why would you be ashamed? Your ex is the one who should be ashamed."

Thomasina surprised herself by smiling. She even felt like laughing. The thought of Art Woodson ever feeling shame for anything amused her. "My ex isn't capable of feeling shame. He makes a living off of shaming others. He's a shame expert, and an expert in how to avoid it."

Kade studied the view out the window. The only sound between them was the motor running and U2 singing "I still haven't found what I'm looking for." He didn't speak until the song ended. "So I promised to show you the city lights. You still want to see them?"

"Yes! I'd love that," Thomasina said. She was relieved that Kade offered her an out. The date had started out fun. She wanted very much for it to end on that note, but feared she had just scared Kade off. She didn't know Kade would view as a challenge the things that scared a lesser man away.

He was more intrigued than ever. Who was this woman? And where did she draw her strength? It helped that she was pretty and had an infectious laugh. Kade loved a good time and anyone who liked to laugh.

Once they were up on Sharp's Ridge, they sat on the tailgate of Kade's truck and looked out over Knoxville. Kade cranked up the radio and let the music float out across the valley.

"Locals call it antenna hill 'cause this is where they put the towers for all the radio and TV stations. It makes it kind of ugly if you're looking up that way." He nodded behind them at a grouping of towers with blinking lights. "But if you look this way, it's a beautiful sight. Not like New York or Atlanta, but still pretty."

"It's sparkly," Thomasina said. "Hey, I think I can see the hospital. Is that it?" she pointed.

"I believe so," Kade replied.

They sat up there all night long, talking, snuggling, kissing, and talking some more until a bashful sun began to tease the twilight away. And after that night, they were nearly inseparable.

Kade's home was an upscale loft above a restaurant in downtown Knoxville. Some mornings they would drink coffee out on the balcony where they could watch UT's rowers push and pull their way through the river. Yes, after one blind date, Thomasina had spent numerous nights with this man. She could barely recognize herself, but she liked what she saw!

One morning, Kade rose slowly from the bed. "I'm going to hop in the shower. Care to join me?" Thomasina admired his naked body as he walked across the bedroom, stepping over their clothes.

"Mmm. Maybe," she said, smiling. "Or maybe you could just stand there for a moment longer and let me enjoy the view."

Kade laughed. "It's all better close up. C'mon, join me. You can't beat a walk-in shower with a bench. You can have a front-row seat. They're the best."

"Okay," Thomasina replied. "You've convinced me." She tossed the sheets back. Kade admired her full breasts, noting their blush in the gentle sway as she walked towards him. Cupping them with both hands, he bent over and kissed her nipples. First one, then the other. Then, pulling her in, Kade's tongue traced a trail upwards to her mouth.

It had been a long time since Kade had known this sort of hunger. The kind that makes a man crazed, blind, never satiated, always starving for more of that one woman. If either of his former wives had that kind of effect on Kade, he had no memory of it. Perhaps the divorces had dulled his senses toward them. As Thomasina reached for him, the phone rang.

"Sorry," Kade said. "Sorry, I'm on call. I have to take it." Gesturing toward the shower, he grabbed a towel for himself. "Go ahead," he told her. Thomasina turned on the water, adjusting the knobs. The shower filled with steam, blocking her from sight.

Kade grabbed the receiver of the hall phone. "Yeah?"

"You gotta come in, right away," his boss said.

"Right now?"

"Yeah, right now."

"What's going on?" Kade asked.

"Attempted murder, possible murder. I'll fill you in when you get here."

"Yeah. Alright."

"You're twenty minutes away. I expect you to be here in twenty-five minutes."

"I was about to shower," Kade snapped. "I'll be there as soon as I can."

"Well, get off the phone and hurry the hell up," his boss replied.

Thomasina was still in the shower when Kade stepped in. He joined her under the showerhead and kissed her longingly. She soaped his back, his belly, between his legs. Kade pulled away. "Sorry," he said. "No time to linger. Duty calls." He rinsed off quickly and stepped back out. She turned off the shower and wrapped her hair in a towel Kade handed her.

"I'll leave the house key in the tray on that hallway table, next to the phone," he said, pulling on his pants. "Just lock up when you leave."

"Okay," she said. "Anything else?"

"Feel free to stay as long as you like, but I don't have any idea when I'll be back."

"Call me."

Kade strapped on his holster and pulled a black t-shirt over it. He sat on the bed and tied up his boots. "I will," he said. Standing, he cupped her face in his hands and gave her a quick kiss on the forehead. "Soon as I'm able."

After Kade drove away, Thomasina fixed a cup of coffee, made the bed, picked up Kade's clothes strewn about the floor, and put them in the clothes hamper. Then she shook her hair out and hung the towel in the bathroom.

Smiling, she slipped into her jeans and a faded tee, then rinsed out her coffee cup and left it turned upside down to dry. If she had her druthers, she would have spent the entire day relaxing about Kade's well-appointed apartment. She especially loved his collection of Walter Anderson art. Her favorite was a painting of cormorants perched on pilings overlooking a bay. There was something protective about the uniform way the birds lined up, as if taunting the wind or the water to try to separate them. Kade had said the birds reminded him of the people in the mountain community where he grew up, always watching out for one another, braving the storms of life together no matter what.

Thomasina had no idea what it was like to have a whole community of people to lean on. The best she'd been able to do was cobble together a friend here and there, and her sons, well, at least one of them. But, as she told Kade, most people she knew huddled around whoever had the most money, the best toys. Once she broke away from her abusive marriage, Thomasina learned to make her own way in the world. She'd warned Kade that most of the time she flew solo.

This sense of independence and aloneness underscored Anderson's art and made it resonate with Thomasina, especially once she learned that the artist struggled with mental illness. There had been times during her marriage when Thomasina thought she might lose her mind. That experience had softened her heart to anyone who dealt with the instability of mental illness.

Kade had encouraged her to read the coffee table book he had on Walter Anderson. So she had and learned that Anderson, a New Orleans native born at the turn of the century, was raised by parents intent on transforming their three sons—Walter and his two brothers—into artists. The family maintained a successful pottery business, Shearwater Pottery, in Ocean Springs, Mississippi, that was still in operation. Tragically, as talented as he was, Anderson suffered manic spells that made him a frightening creature to those who loved him best. Reading about Anderson's madness caused Thomasina to think about the ways in which mania manifests itself, how it can compel some, like Anderson, to create, and some, like her ex-husband, to destroy. Anderson had been able to capture the fragility and the strength of the cormorants, translating that juxtaposition into his work.

Thomasina felt like she was a juxtaposition herself. Since leaving Baltimore, she had found it difficult to be in relationships. She was unwilling, and often truly unable, to allow herself to be vulnerable. She wanted to be strong but found that fear always shrinks the world people inhabit. Yet there were the cormorants, in all of their feathered fragility, flapping about the big wide world with abandon. Thomasina wanted to be free like that. She didn't want her past experiences to define her future ones. If she couldn't move about the world freely, with fearlessness and joy, then her ex would continue to control her from afar. And Thomasina couldn't stand the thought of giving Art Woodson another minute of her life.

Grabbing her purse and the key that Kade left for her, Thomasina headed out. She had a meeting at the hospital at 1 p.m. and needed to run some errands beforehand. Terry's birthday was coming up, and she wanted to get a card and check in the mail to him. She'd quit buying gifts for him and Douglas, figuring they'd rather just have the money to use as they willed. She had not yet introduced Kade to Douglas, although her son knew she was seeing somebody.

Their relationship had moved faster than either Kade or Thomasina could have imagined. Thomasina counted backwards through the weeks of October and September. Five weeks, maybe more. Was this the real thing?

She pulled up in front of the post office. As she sat in her car, writing a check to her eldest son, the local public broadcast station followed Prairie Home Companion with a news report that a man had been life-flighted from a remote region of Hawkins County to UT's Medical Center after falling from the top of a waterfall. She figured he would be lucky if he managed to live through the night. Thomasina knew that few people survived such accidents.

She was unaware that Creed's fall was no accident.

Chapter 17

The phone in Conley's office buzzed. He pushed the flashing red light and picked up the receiver.

"What is it now, Darlene?" Conley snapped at his assistant. Mr. Bone, who ran the produce market, had been calling all morning because he'd discovered a crop circle in one of his fields. He was sure it was a sign of the Apocalypse and wanted Conley to get out to his place as quickly as possible, or at least before the reporters from the newspaper and TV stations arrived.

"It's not Mr. Bone this time," she said. "It's Vaughnell. She said it's urgent that she speak to you."

"Which line is she on?" Every light on the phone was blinking.

"Line three," Darlene replied.

Conley pushed the button. "Whatcha need, Vaughnell?"

"It ain't me who's doing the needing," she answered. "Why are you in such a foul mood anyway?"

"I'm not in a foul mood," Conley protested. "Must be my natural sunny disposition shining through."

"You're full of shit."

"Probably, but that's a personal matter. What can I do you for?"

"I got something for you on the shooting at Laidlow's."

"You do?" Conley grabbed a pen and pad. "What is it?"

"Last night I had this dream…"

"C'mon Vaughnell. I ain't got time for no dream shit. I need something more concrete. Ain't you got a crystal ball, some tea leaves?"

"I'm gonna hang up if you don't show me some respect. You asked for my help. I'm trying to give it to you."

Conley shifted the receiver to his other shoulder. "I'm sorry. Go ahead. I'm all ears." He took a sip of coffee and grimaced. It had gone cold.

"Well, you know, I get these dreams sometimes. Usually, they come right before something awful happens. Like the time Frankie Feagin's barn burnt down with all that hay. You remember that? I'd called and warned him the week before that a fire was coming."

"Uh-huh," Conley said. Much as he wanted Vaughnell to get to the point, he knew that if he made one more snide remark about needing her to hurry up, she would never tell him what she saw in her dream. Vaughnell could be a capricious woman when she wanted to be.

"I don't rightly know how to tell you this."

"Just spit it out."

"I had this dream and you and Clive were in it."

"Me and Clive? What's that got to do with Laidlow's?"

"I don't know," she said. "That's the part you have to figure out."

"Vaughnell, you ain't making any sense."

"Well, I might if you let me finish."

"Go ahead."

"You and Clive were on your way to Laidlow's in your car. You were going to pick up some more of his pain meds. Only on the way there, Clive jumped out of the car and started running away, like he was scared of you for some reason." Vaughnell stopped talking, waited.

"That's it?" Conley asked. He pushed the pen and notepad aside. "That's all you got?"

"Yeah. I woke up after that. My heart was beating a gazillion miles a minute, like I was the one doing the running or something."

Conley shook his head. Rubbed his hand over his mid-morning stubble. He didn't know whether to cuss Vaughnell or thank her and hope she'd go away. He was about to settle on the latter, when Vaughnell added, "You need to be careful, cousin. You are in danger."

"Danger? How am I in danger?"

"I don't rightly know," she replied. "Sometimes when I have these dreams, I wake up with this feeling. Sometimes the feeling is more telling than the dream itself. And this morning, the feeling concerned you. I have this impression, if you will, that's something is seriously wrong. Have you had a checkup lately?"

"A checkup?"

"Yeah. You know, have you seen a doctor? Had your heart checked? Blood pressure?"

Conley couldn't contain his frustration any longer.

"Lord, Vaughnell, sometimes I think you spend too much time in that garden of yours. You might have suffered a heat stroke or something."

"I got to go," she said. "You can heed the warning or not. That's up to you, but I am not going to tolerate your ugliness about it."

"Oh, c'mon, Vaughnell. You know I didn't mean nothing by it," Conley said. "You have to admit, it's a crazy story you're telling me."

"Maybe so," Vaughnell replied. "But that don't mean there's not truth to it." She hung up before Conley could say another word. He sat there holding the receiver, unsure whether to hang up or to call his doctor for an appointment.

Chapter 18

Zeb had never allowed himself to consider the possibility of returning to Christian Bend. He'd made a new life in Bayeux, and while many may have found his daily routine boring, confining even, Zeb took comfort in its rhythms. When you'd been to war, seen the things Zeb had seen, done the things Zeb had done, you came to appreciate a quiet and orderly life.

He kept his circle of friends small and tight. They knew that something bad had happened to "Le Sammy," as they called him, but they had no idea what, and thankfully for Zeb, they were too polite to ask. While he had not yet forgiven himself, he had learned to forgive God for the death of Sgt. Harootunian, for Rain's deafness, for Maizee's suicide.

Much of this healing had come as Zeb prepared for Baptism, and Confirmation in the Catholic Church. That time of refection and ongoing talks with Father Thom had enabled Zeb to see that much of the sorrows of the world were the result of man's actions and not God's neglect.

Zeb had been baptized in the church in Christian Bend, but like everything else about his life there, it seemed like a story he'd read long ago instead of a life he'd once led. When his confirmation was complete, Zeb did feel like a different person. Not a new man, but a man who found a new grace.

Perhaps the most noticeable difference, at least to Zeb, was an awakening of gratitude. Although he'd never quit missing Maizee and Rain and the life they all had prior to the war, Zeb had become thankful for his life in Bayeux, for Father Thom and the friendship they'd forged from a landscape of loss. Bayeux and its people had welcomed Zeb; they gave him work and a home, and, most of all, they gave him daily kindnesses. It was those kindnesses—the smiles, the handshakes, the loaves of bread and berry pies, the jokes shared over mugs of cider—that enabled Zeb to put away the pains of the past.

It wasn't a matter of "getting over" all that he had endured as much as it was coming to a place of resignation, an acknowledgment that nothing would ever be okay—not Maizee's death or Rain's disability, not Sarge's death, and, worst of all, not the killing of that young boy. None of any of it would ever be okay.

Still, with Father Thom's help, Zeb had learned to make a way forward. He had carved out a life for himself among the ancient stone of Bayeux. Where else might a man with a heart hardened by the loss of war be at home but in a city built of stone? Bayeux provided Zeb with refuge. The veteran felt safe walking its narrow cobblestoned streets and praying under the soaring arches of its fortressed cathedral.

Zeb never planned to leave Bayeux. Not until the day Clint found him in the library and told him about Burdy gone missing. If there was anyone Zeb owed something to—and in truth, there were plenty—there was none more so than Burdy. She had given Zeb and Maizee a place to call home when they were just starting out. When Zeb enlisted after the attack on Pearl Harbor, she had given her word that she would do her best to take care of Maizee and Rain. Burdy had faithfully corresponded with Zeb, giving him news from home and news of his boy, as Maizee grew too sick to do so. And even though Maizee took her life, that didn't mean Burdy had failed to keep her promise. Burdy had done everything within her power to prevent the suicide; Zeb was sure of that.

Clint stopped by the bistro after the lunch crowd thinned out and let Zeb know that his assistant had made the travel arrangements. They would fly from Paris into New York City, where they'd rent a car and drive down to Tennessee. They had hotel reservations in Kingsport.

"And you still can't reach Burdy?" Zeb asked.

Clint nodded. "You don't have to go with me," he said. "I can do this alone."

"I know you can," Zeb said. "But I want to go."

"You sure?" Clint's eyebrows lifted.

Zeb circled the top of his coffee cup with his forefinger. "I'd be lying if I said I was sure, so no, I'm not sure at all. But I owe it to Burdy. I'm at least sure of that."

Clint thought to mention Rain, to ask how Zeb would handle seeing his boy again, a grown man, after all these years, but he decided against it. Why borrow trouble when there was enough to deal with already? Who knew what would happen once they arrived? Clint wasn't even sure they'd find what had become of Burdy, much less a boy who was now a man.

"I'll pick you up Monday at noon then. Our flight is at 7 p.m. That should give us plenty of time to get checked in."

Zeb hadn't been in a plane since that fateful day of June 6, 1944. He didn't say anything to Clint about it, but the thought of getting back on a plane was more terrifying to him than the thought of anything that might happen once he arrived back in Christian Bend. Well, maybe not more terrifying, but equally so. His stomach was one big knot of nerves. What had he gotten himself into?

"See you Monday," Zeb said. He opened the bistro door for Clint, who offered a backhand wave as he walked down the street toward the corner market.

Chapter 19

Burdy had watched from the back door as Rain headed up the hillside toward Horseshoe Falls, and when he didn't come down in a timely fashion, she feared something had happened. What she'd really feared is that Rain, angry with her, angry with Zeb, may have done the unthinkable, may have jumped from the Falls himself.

Burdy knew that her fears had gotten the better of her, but there was no way she was going to risk Rain following in his mother's footsteps. When he took off up that mountain, she perched herself in a chair on the back porch, watching and listening the entire time he was gone.

She was sitting there still when she heard his yells echoing down through the mountain laurel and maples. She couldn't make out what he was yelling, but she recognized the sound of terror when she heard it. She called the sheriff right away and told him what she feared, that a young man had gone up on the mountain and may have jumped from Horseshoe Falls. "Send somebody quick," Burdy demanded. "Hurry."

She would have gone up after Rain her own self if not for her bum leg. She could barely get out to the back porch with that walker contraption of hers, so she knew there was no way she'd be able to get across the backyard and up the hillside. Tibbis must be thinking she'd plum forgotten about him; she hadn't been up to the gravehouse in a month of Sundays or longer. But there was time for that, and she knew Tibbis would forgive her. Right now, Rain was her concern.

A couple of deputies found Rain next to a boulder, soaking wet and cradling Creed, giving him mouth-to-mouth resuscitation, doing most of his breathing for him. They called for an emergency crew who airlifted Creed straight off the mountain and carried him to Knoxville. The deputies draped a blanket over Rain and led him down the slopes.

They give Rain over to Burdy, but not before getting as much information from him as he could recall: Two men fighting atop the Falls too close to the edge. One had fallen. Or maybe he was pushed? Rain couldn't be sure. He didn't see it. Or if he did see, he couldn't remember. No. He didn't know who the other man was. Rain hadn't even known the first man was Creed until it was too late. He couldn't make out most of what the men were yelling about, but he was pretty sure he'd heard one of them say something about "Bean Station."

Burdy helped mediate the conversation between Rain and the deputies, since they were unfamiliar with his speech patterns. Those patterns were far more pronounced when Rain was distressed or agitated, and he was both when he came off that mountain.

"I think he's answered enough questions for now, fellas," Burdy finally said. She poured Rain a cup of warm brew to help settle his nerves. "You can call back tomorrow." Burdy walked the deputies to the front door, giving them no opportunity to argue with her. "You all gonna go out to Creed's house and let his daddy know?" They assured her they would. "Well, soon as you hear something about his condition, call me, okay?"

"Yes, ma'am," the deputy said.

The younger fella handed Burdy a backpack. "This here belongs to your friend. His sleeping bag is still on the mountain, but I picked this up."

"Thank you," Burdy said. She took the bag and slipped it over the handle of her walker. "And please tell Boog—Creed's daddy—to call me if he needs anything."

When Burdy returned to the kitchen, Rain was sitting at the table drinking his second cup of tea.

"What's in this stuff?" he asked. He looked up at Burdy, saw the backpack hanging from her walker.

"Ginseng and some blackberry moonshine," Burdy replied. "A few other things, but mostly those." She dropped the backpack into the chair next to Rain. "Deputy said he picked this up. Said he believed it was your'n."

Rain nodded. "Yep."

The bag had only been half-zipped. Burdy saw Zeb's letters inside.

She poured herself a cup of tea and sat across from Rain. "You read them yet?"

Rain shook his head. The tension between them made the air thick. They were both finding it difficult to draw deep breath. "I took 'em up there with me. I was getting ready to read them when all that commotion got underway." Rain avoided looking at Burdy. He couldn't help it. Whenever he was in her presence, he reverted to the boy she'd loved with abandon, the boy who had loved her back just as fiercely. He was mad with her still, so mad, but he couldn't disrespect her, as much as he wanted to. "Where's Wheedin?" he asked, trying to focus on something different.

"She went back to Greeneville, had some meetings she had to tend to. She's coming back tomorrow, but I'm able to do for myself."

"I see that."

"There's some of Tibbis's clothes hanging in the chifforobe, if you're wanting to put some dry clothes on."

"Naw. I'm mostly dry now. And warm, too, thanks to you." Rain held up his half-empty teacup. The tea had at least helped take the edge off his anger. Or maybe he was just too tired to work up any fury. Either way, Rain didn't want to leave. He wanted to believe that Burdy could fix this, the way she'd always fixed so many hurting people all over Christian Bend. "I do need something from you, though."

The comment startled Burdy. She didn't think there would ever come a day when Rain needed anything from her, except maybe an apology. "What, honey? What do you need from me?"

"I need to understand."

"I'm not sure I can help you with that, Rain. I'm not sure I understand it all myself."

"Why did you lie to me about my dad?"

"Oh, honey, it wasn't a lie."

Rain stared at Burdy as if she were on fire. She and Leela-Ma and Doc had been the moral compass that set his entire world. He thought the sun would fall from the sky before any one of them would lie to him. "Don't make me cuss."

Burdy got up and pulled out a quart jar of shine from the cupboard, poured her cup full, and refilled Rain's. "You're right," she said, sitting back down and taking a long sip from her cup. "What I did was deceitful. I was living a lie even if I wasn't telling one. I am so sorry, Rain. I wasn't trying to hurt you. I was trying to do everything I could to keep that from happening. It's more complicated than you think."

"You don't know what I think!" Rain lashed out.

Burdy took the lashing in silence. She figured she deserved it. "I don't know how to make things right between us," she said finally.

"You could start by telling me the truth."

"How much of the truth do you want to know?"

"All of it."

"You sure about that?"

Rain drained the last sip from his cup before he answered. "Mind if I use your bathroom?"

"Go on. Help yo'self."

Rain relieved himself, washed his hands and his face. Standing before the mirror clouded with age, Rain tried to tame the angry boy within. The extra dose of alcohol now seemed to have the opposite effect. His anger was growing. "You sure, son?" he asked himself. The boy answered back with a fury common to those who've discovered a betrayal: "Hell, yeah!"

Rain returned to the kitchen to find his father's letters splayed out across the table and Burdy shuffling through them as if searching through a deck of cards for the Jack of Hearts. The Christ card, a sign of twisted fate. Surely fitting of Rain's life. His parents' lives, too, although Rain didn't yet know how true that was.

"Here it is." Burdy held up an airmail envelope, yellowed with age. She nodded to the empty chair where Rain had been moments before. "Sit down."

Rain did as he was told. "What is it?"

"This"—she sliced the envelope through the air—"is the first letter I ever received from your father." She studied the faded postmark. "June 21, 1956. Yes, that's the first one. I remember the day it came. Little Fern Campbell met me on my way home. She had her Mason jar out and was searching for lightning bugs.

"You remember the Campbell girl? Sweet child, but Lord Gawd a'mercy that girl could talk the hind-end off a mule. It's a shame what came of her, broke her mama's heart."

Rain didn't really remember the girl, but he asked the question Burdy was expecting from him: "What happened to her?"

"She got that New York city disease."

Rain shrugged his shoulders and shook his head, letting Burdy know that he was unaware of any disease associated with a city.

"You know. That disease killing all them queer fellas up in New York City."

"You mean AIDS?"

"That's the one," Burdy said. "An awful disease. Fern died last year right there on a bed in her momma's living room. I offered

121

whatever comforts I could but my remedies were no match for that withering disease. You knowed anyone to die from it?"

Rain shook his head.

"Well, you don't want to neither. Trust me. Poor Fern didn't weigh no more than sixty-two pounds when she died. She was just a bird of a woman by the time the end come around.

"She was working at some magazine up in New York City when she fell ill. Mrs. Campbell said it was Fern's boyfriend who gave the disease to her, but I don't think anybody rightly knows how she got it. Mrs. Campbell went up there and carried her home when she got too ill to care for herself.

"They's some at the church and around town wouldn't go around Mrs. Campbell once she brought Fern home. They were scared they'd get the disease, too. Foolishness was all that was. People who live afraid of everything ain't really living at all."

Rain had been as patient as possible. "What's all this stuff with Fern got to do with that letter in your hand?"

Burdy was taken aback. Being blunt wasn't Rain's way. "Well, nothing. I was just saying I'd run into little Fern Campbell the day the letter came. A person doesn't forget a day like that."

"No, I don't expect so," Rain replied.

"I want you to understand that up until I got this letter from your daddy, I figured him for dead just the same as you. Everybody did. I had no reason to expect he was alive. They never returned his body, but that's war for you. The Army told us your daddy was gone. Over ten years had passed and none of us had heard a word from him, until I got this letter.

"You want me to read it to you?"

Rain nodded an affirmation. He rubbed his sweating hands over his thighs, cupped them around his knees.

"Okay, then." Burdy unfolded the letter. It was written on paper so thin it looked like the Elmer's glue skin that Rain and his classmates made in grade school whenever they found a bottle of glue that hadn't dried up. He could see his father's handwriting through the back of the paper as Burdy held it up. He'd never seen his father's handwriting before. As she read aloud, Rain felt like he was hearing Zeb's voice. A voice he had not heard since he was a toddler. It was both comforting and unsettling.

Burdy,
I have written this letter a thousand times in my head. This is the first time I've actually put the pen to paper. I don't yet know if I have the courage to drop this in the mail.

I don't even know if it would be courage, or plain foolishness. I can't seem to settle the matter in my mind. Courage isn't the only thing I can't reconcile in my head anymore.

Most days I think it is best to let everyone go on thinking I am dead. A lot of the time, I feel so numbed I might as well be. Just because a man is breathing don't make him alive.

I'd appreciate it if you wouldn't mention this letter to Maizee or Leela. I'd like you to keep it between the two of us for now. But if you aren't too put out, I'd appreciate it if you would write back and tell me how Rain is doing.

Rain didn't know what he'd expected, but this wasn't it. He realized that his father wasn't even aware that Maizee had taken her own life. How could he have known? Who would have told him?

Burdy continued reading:

You can write to me care of The Cathedral of Notre-Dame, 4 Rue du Général de Dais, 14400 Bayeux, France. I know I owe you an explanation. Maybe one day, if I can ever get it sorted out enough in my own mind, I'll be able to explain it to you.

Zeb

When she finished, Burdy folded the letter and put it back in the faded envelope. She'd stacked all the letters by postmark date. Picking up the next one in the pile, she asked, "Do you want me to keep going?"

"Wait!" Rain held up his hand. "Does he know?" Anguish creased his forehead, his eyes.

"Does he know what, Baby?" Burdy replied. She'd called him Baby all his life whenever she was feeling particularly protective of him.

"About my mother?"

She nodded. "He does now. He didn't know it when he wrote that letter."

"You? Are you the one who told him?"

"Yes," Burdy replied. "I told him."

"When? When did you tell him?" Rain spoke harshly, commandingly, as if she were his hired help messing up a job he'd given her to do. There was a fire raging through his bones that, if left unchecked, he was pretty sure it would consume them both. It was anger, yes, but it was something more than that—a longing denied. The little boy inside of Rain still longed for the father he'd lost.

"Years ago," Burdy answered. She did not raise her voice, did not get defensive. She accepted Rain's rage, even if she didn't completely understand it. "On my first trip to France."

"Wait! What? You went to France?"

Burdy nodded. "Many times, but the first time was shortly after I received this letter. I went to find your daddy, to try and figure out how come he had abandoned you and your mother."

Unable to control his rage any longer, Rain dropped his head and began to sob. It was an awful wracking cry, the kind usually only heard from unseen animals after midnight in deep woods.

Rain's belly heaved, his shoulders shuddered. He was freezing cold on the outside and fiery hot within. Recognizing that he was in a state of shock, Burdy grabbed an afghan from the living room and wrapped it around him.

She put a tin bucket beside him just seconds before he leaned over and heaved up the contents of his stomach, mostly shine and herbs. Burdy pulled a chair alongside him, handed him a warm wash cloth.

"Baby, I am so very sorry. I should have told you. I meant to tell you. I am so sorry."

Rain continued that hard crying for a good twenty minutes, maybe longer. From where she sat next to him, Burdy thought his crying seemed an eternal thing, without form and without finality.

It didn't bother her to see a man weep. She'd borne witness to that many times over the years, especially when she was working the tuberculosis ward at Pressmen's. Burdy knew that Rain, like his momma before him, kept all his sorrows swallowed up on the inside. Far as she knew, Rain had never grieved for his mother, much less his daddy. She just sat there, praying quietly as Rain wept. Praying for physical strength for the both of them, wisdom for her, and repentance for her part in hurting Rain further.

He stopped crying as suddenly as he had begun. Water on. Water off. He picked up the pail where he'd vomited, carried it out back, and cleaned it with the water hose. Then he put the pail back on the porch. Burdy stood at the back door and watched him through the screen.

Afterward, he pulled a cigarette from his shirt pocket. He didn't smoke as a habit, but something about being back in the hills compelled him. He tapped out an extra one and offered it to Burdy.

"Naw, I better not," she said. "Old women like me can't afford the extravagancies of our youth no more."

"Suit yourself," Rain replied. He lit his with a lighter, careful not to hold it too close lest the blue flames singe his brows and lashes. He sat on the stoop and studied the orange tip of his smoke.

"If you want me to read you any more of these letters, you'll have to come back inside," Burdy said.

"I don't want to hear any more from those letters."

"You don't?"

"No," Rain said. "What I want is for you to tell me what's in them. I want you to tell me why my father quit on us." Rain's voice cracked under the weight of his words.

"Oh, Baby, your father didn't quit on you," Burdy said. "It's not like that." She opened the screen door and with great care moved to the rocker and sat down.

Then, in a hushed, small voice underneath the faraway lightning bugs of the dark heavens, Burdy told Rain the story of the father he lost to war, and of the broken man who could not return to the woman and child he loved still.

When she finished her story, Burdy stood up and made her way back into the house. Rain helped her manage the stairs, and then, towering over her, he leaned down and kissed the top of her white head.

"I'm sorry for being so hateful to you these past couple of months, Burdy." Rain's cheeks were luminescent underneath the porch light. Cleansing tears, the kind only repentant sinners shed, lit up his face.

"It's my fault," she replied, her face glistening, too. "I should have told you. Don't hate me. And don't hate your dad. The pain of war remains with all of us long after the bombing stops."

Rain walked across the yard between the two houses, thinking about Burdy's parting words and the lasting pain of war.

Not bothering to undress, he fell asleep that night atop the bed where his momma had given birth to him on a hot August night so long ago. On that same bed a year or so later, on a frigid winter's night, his father, under Burdy's direction, had bathed the child in the cleanest snow he could find. All in an effort to break the fever that robbed Rain of a lot of his hearing and threatened his life.

Rain only knew those stories because Burdy had always been more than willing to share them. Doc and Leela-Ma would share them, too, but it was always harder for them. Hard, too, for Rain to ask. Somehow, Burdy always knew how much Rain needed to hear the tales of when he was a boy, of when they were a family. It was the stories Burdy shared that kept his mother and his father present.

For the first time in years, Rain prayed in earnest, thanking God that he'd always had parents and a community of people who loved him deeply. Before falling asleep, he even said a prayer of forgiveness for the father who abandoned him all those years ago.

That night his dreams were not haunted with the voices of his mother or the cries for his father. That night Rain dreamt of Mary Esther. It was a deep sleep, a healing sleep, filled with longings of a different sort.

Chapter 20

The road east had more curves than Marilyn Monroe, Kade thought as he leaned the Trans Am into another narrow bend along Tennessee's Bloody Eleven. A log truck coming from the other direction began to drift. Kade laid into the horn, hoping to startle the driver awake. The driver pulled his truck back into his own lane. As they passed one another, Kade reached his hand out the window and flipped off the driver.

The logger recognized the one-finger salute with a nod.

"Damn truckers think they own the road," Kade said. Talking to himself while driving was one of his coping mechanisms. It helped him to relieve some of the pressures of the job. Kade hated the way drugs, legal and illegal, were changing the landscape of his childhood.

"And people thought shine was bad," Kade thought out loud. "It wasn't nearly as bad as what we're dealing with now."

As he drove along the fertile flatlands that spread out from Richland Creek, Kade thought back to when every farmer grew a plot of tobacco and kept a still hidden someplace on the property. It seemed strange to want to go back to such times, but he did.

And yet there was still beauty in the world. As far up the road as he could see, a patchwork of red and gold trees stretched out before him. The beauty of the hills never escaped Kade. He considered himself a fortunate son, to have been born in these mountains, to be a part of the community of hardscrabble people, fierce in their loyalties to one another and to the land.

He scanned the run-down houses as he drove by. A boy, three or four years of age, walked barefoot across a gravel drive, yanking a coffee can on a string behind him, a makeshift pet. A woman sat underneath a tree in a ladder-back chair, her heavy thighs spilling down around her like too much pudding in a bowl. She was yelling at the boy, but Kade couldn't make out what she was saying over the air blowing in his window.

Poor as church mice, his momma used to say. Too poor to quit and too proud to whitewash, his daddy would respond. They talked about this neighbor or that one, always aware that they were just one paycheck away from total devastation themselves.

Kade's own granny got by on the "government check" that came once a month—Social Security. It wasn't but a few hundred dollars, but it was enough to pay the light bill and buy groceries. She still lived in Rogersville in the shotgun house her parents built, the house where she and all her siblings were born. Medical care wasn't a luxury his people could afford. As a matter of fact, Kade was the first in his family to have health insurance and a retirement plan. That made him the wealthiest man among them.

Life in the hills challenged even the hardest-working folks. Lazy people didn't stand a chance at survival without turning to some sort of criminal behavior. And, as Kade knew all too well, the region's changing culture and influx of drugs created a whole new class of people too doped up to work. They lived for the party and the next day's high. They were a breed of people separate from their ancestors who had settled these hills.

Spoiled, his granny called it. Sorry, his mama said. No-counts, his daddy suggested. Kade preferred to consider them misguided. He was less concerned with how they got to the place they did than with figuring out how to put a roadblock in their wayward paths and convince them to turn their lives around.

He'd never been seduced by drugs; Kade had no interest in getting high through some artificial means. If he needed a high, he could just pick up his guitar and strum a tune. Or he might bring his fishing pole over to Cherokee Lake and spend the day on the boat, trolling. He didn't even care if he caught anything.

"I need to bring Thomasina out here," he told himself as he passed the lake.

But first things first. Kade had a job to do. He had spoken with the police chief at Bean Station yesterday, calling Chief Conley shortly after he left the hospital where Creed McPheters lay unconscious, a machine doing his breathing for him. So it wasn't Creed who alerted Kade to something badly amiss. He wasn't able to alert anybody about anything. It was Creed's daddy instead. Kade sighed as he replayed their conversation.

Boog had been at his son's side when Kade arrived at the hospital. The old man was wheeling around an oxygen tank of his own, his skin pale as mold on a slice of bread gone bad. His angular face was drawn down, grief-stricken, and his long hands had crusty white scabs on the knuckles, some sort of skin disorder that Kade didn't recognize. The poor man cried with every word he uttered.

And he had a lot of them. He told Kade he was sure that the person responsible for his son's fall was a fellow named Clive Conley.

"What makes you think that?" Kade asked. He had taken a small recorder out of his pocket and held it between them as Boog spoke.

"That Clive fella and Creed had some kind of business deal going on."

"What kind of business?"

"A bad kind," Boog replied.

Of course, Kade already knew what Boog was confirming. The DEA had been conducting their own investigation into drug running throughout the region. Just a week ago, they'd arrested a fellow over at Poor Valley Knobs who had taken his own twelve-year-old niece hostage.

The man, high on something, took the girl from her grandmother's home at gunpoint. He tied up the grandmother and

130

threatened to kill her. The drug-addled man took the girl by van to a remote wooded area up past Newman's Ridge. Over the course of the three weeks it took law enforcement to find the two of them, he repeatedly raped and tortured the child.

While working for the DEA, Kade encountered more abused children than decent people could conceive of. If Kade had been aware when he began the job that it would include the kind of depravity he'd come to know, he never would have made it his career.

The Tennessee Kade grew up in was a community of people caring for and taking care of each other. Drugs changed all that. Kids were more vulnerable than ever.

Drug abuse had taken over the state, stripped it of its family values and pride, and left thousands of neglected and abused children in its wake. There weren't enough state funds or workers to address the burden that resulted from addicted parents. Children became the currency by which drug-addled parents and state stakeholders bartered. It both sickened Kade and undergirded his resolve to do all within his power to stop it.

Governor McWheter, in an effort to combat the growing epidemic of drug abuse, took the historic step of unifying all the state's resources under the Alliance for a Drug Free Tennessee. While Kade appreciated McWheter's efforts and the millions he was allocating at the local level, he suspected the efforts were at least a decade too late. When it came to money and resources, drug smugglers were way ahead.

A month or so earlier, Kade had been called out to the site of a plane crash on an old abandoned airport in Sullivan County. Agents recovered 400 pounds of marijuana from the wreckage. The deceased pilot was a popular radiologist with a good job that paid well, but smuggling drugs made him even richer. He and another childhood friend had been running drugs for a couple of years.

His friend, who had watched him die in the crash, was caught about ten miles away when a cop pulled him over for a missing headlight on his truck. The truck bed was loaded with an additional 200 pounds of marijuana, completely uncovered. Combined, the marijuana had a street value of about $400,000, and that was just a small, two-man outfit. Every county in the state had at least one such operation underway. There was a lot of money being made in the drug-running business.

It turned out that the man over at Poor Valley Knobs who took his niece hostage identified his supplier to the agents, and when the agents followed up on that information, it led right to Creed McPheters.

Kade didn't have all the details down yet, but it was shaping up to look as though Creed and this Conley friend of his were involved in a drug-smuggling operation of their own. Boog McPheters told Kade about the marijuana his son had on his property. Creed and this Conley friend had a crop of regular customers they served. And they weren't all locals, neither, Boog told Kade. The two was running the stuff up and down the interstate, through Tennessee, Georgia, and on into Florida. It was certain that Creed's "accident" at the falls wasn't an accident at all. And now Kade had to talk to the father of Creed's apparent accomplice.

Chapter 21

Kade pulled his car into a spot marked "Visitor," although he wondered why the designation was needed in a little place like Bean Station. It was likely that if you weren't from Bean Station, any onlookers would be able to ascertain that in a matter of seconds. And besides, it wasn't like the parking lot outside Chief Conley's office was busy.

A lone cop car sat in the space underneath the only tree providing any shade. "My granny would probably refuse to drive that, at least without a stuffed pink snake in the back window," Kade said, chuckling to himself. He figured the Crown Victoria had to be at least seven years old, and there had to be one more just like it out on patrol right now.

"The Chief is expecting you," Darlene said when Kade handed her his business card. "Go on in."

Chief Conley stood up and reached across the desk to shake Kade's hand.

"Have a seat," he said.

Kade looked at the chair's cracked grey Naugahyde and said, "You don't mind if I stand, do you? Long drive over. My hind end is starting to cramp on me."

"Suit yourself," the Chief said. "What can I do you for?"

This would be no casual conversation, and both men understood that. The Chief wasn't happy to have a federal agent snooping around his neighborhood, though he wasn't clear on exactly what Kade wanted. He'd just called yesterday and said he'd be dropping by. Never said why.

"You have any new information on that shooting over at the pharmacy?" Kade asked.

"I might have," the Chief said. He did not sit back down, figuring if Kade was going to stand, he would too. He wasn't going to give the fed fella an inch of ground on his home turf. "Is that what you drove all the way up here for? Why would your agency be interested in the Laidlow incident?"

Kade knew more than he was willing to let on, so he took a diversionary approach. "I had a friend injured in that incident."

"Mrs. Luttrell?"

"Yeah."

"How's she doing?" Chief Conley walked over to the window and stared out. He wished he had a better idea of who was behind the Laidlow killings, but the truth was that he was out of his league on this case. He had so little to go on, mostly eyewitness accounts, and those were unreliable given the gear the killer wore to hide his identity.

"She went home a few weeks ago. I'm headed up there soon to check in on her."

"Detective Wiley was out there not long ago to interview her." Chief Conley pulled out a cigarette. "Mind if I smoke?"

"It's your office," Kade said with a shrug.

Conley flipped his Zippo open and lit his cig. "Detective Wiley said the old woman might not be herself."

"What do you mean?" Kade asked.

"She can't remember anything. Or not much of anything to do with the shootings."

"Well, that wouldn't be so unusual, would it?" Kade remarked. "I would think a lot of people might forget a trauma like that."

"Maybe so," Conley replied.

"Lemme ask you something," Kade said.

Conley dumped half a cup of stale coffee out the open window into the pebble rock below. "Sure."

"Your boy, Clive, do you know where I can find him?"

"Clive?" Chief Conley was taken aback. "What business do you have with him?"

"Personal," Kade replied. "Do you know how I can reach him? I've called his phone, left messages for him at home, but he hasn't returned any of them. If I didn't know better, I might think he was trying to avoid me."

Chief Conley walked back to his desk and sat down, no longer interested in posturing with Kade. He was actually feeling a bit weak in the bones. He mashed out the butt end of his cigarette into the empty coffee cup.

"He's not avoiding you, Kade. My boy's out of town. I'm sure he never even received your calls."

Kade felt agitated now. His face flushed down to his collarbone. "Do you know where he's gone?"

"Montana."

"Montana?"

"Yeah."

"How long ago did he leave?"

"Two…maybe three days ago. He came by the house, said he was headed out to Montana to go hunting with a friend."

"What time of day was it?"

"The day was pretty much over. I'd just finished supper. I was listening to the news on TV. President Reagan was talking about the market crash. Why?"

"Did you find it unusual that he would just show up like that, at that time, and announce he was headed to Montana?" Kade was studying Conley, wondering if he was covering for his son, wondering if he knew more than he was admitting. But Conley seemed truly confused by Kade's line of questioning.

"Yeah, it was kind of odd. I didn't even know Clive had friends out West, and he's never been much of a hunter. Plus, I mean, it was getting on dark and he was going to drive to Montana."

"What kind of rig does he drive?" Kade asked. He had opened a notebook and was jotting down the information that Conley gave him.

"A Jeep Cherokee, silver. 1986. Can you tell me what this is all about?"

"Not yet," Kade said. "Do you know the license number?"

"Not off the top of my head. I can get it for you. Is my boy in some kind of trouble?"

"You tell me, Chief. Is he?" Kade narrowed his eyes and stared a hole at Conley. He was convinced the Chief knew more about his son's misdeeds than he wanted to admit.

Conley's eyes darkened. He rubbed the stubble there on his bald head with both hands, clearly in some sort of distress.

Kade pulled the chair closer to Conley's desk, positioned himself directly in front of the Chief, and sat down.

"It's okay," he said. "Tell me what you know."

"Clive's always been a handful from the time he was little," Conley said. "He didn't have much of an attention span, always got in trouble at school for being up out of his desk, talking back to the teacher, that sort of thing.

"Unlike me, he wasn't any good at sports. I was never sure if it was because he lacked coordination or if he just lacked the mental toughness to learn it. Clive was always one to do whatever was easiest."

The phone buzzed. Conley picked it up.

"Sorry to bother you, Chief," Danielle said, "but Vaughnell is on the line. Said it's important that she speak to you right now."

"You tell Vaughnell I'm in a meeting and I'll call her as soon as I'm done. And hold any further calls, Darlene."

"Yes, sir."

Conley put the receiver in the cradle and turned his attention back to Kade. "Like I was saying, Clive was always a handful. His momma and I sent him off to VMI when he was fourteen."

"VMI?"

"Virginia Military Institute," Conley said. "I was already the police chief by then and I just couldn't risk the kind of trouble Clive was headed for. We thought VMI might straighten him out."

"And?" Kade asked. "Did it?"

Chief Conley picked up a pen and began doodling on a notebook in front of him. Kade couldn't make out what he was drawing, but it was clear that Conley was having some internal debate.

"Clive isn't easily deterred from a path of self-destruction," Conley replied. "I don't know if he was using before he went off to VMI. I mean, for sure he was smoking pot before then. I'd caught him myself a time or two. But at some point, Clive moved on. LSD. Cocaine. Heroin. You name it. Clive never met a drug he wouldn't try and didn't like."

"Has he ever been to rehab?" Kade asked.

"I've got two mortgages on a house I've lived in for thirty years," Conley said. He chuckled, though the sound was humorless. "You know how much it costs to get a kid clean?"

Kade shook his head. "I don't have any kids."

"The wife and I could have bought half of Pensacola Beach for what we've paid to try and keep Clive clean." Conley put the pen down, folded his hands as if in prayer, and dropped his chin to his chest. "Lord God Almighty knows we have done everything we can think of to help that boy of ours, but it's like he was born to create chaos."

Silence settled between them like harbor fog. "There's a reason they call this stuff hard truths," Kade thought. He didn't want to keep pressing Conley, but what choice did he have?

"Did Clive ever mention a fella by the name of Creed McPheters?"

"Yeah. I've heard Clive speak of him, but I've never met him. Him and Clive used to go up to the races at Bristol together. Why?"

"Creed's in the Medical Center in Knoxville hooked up to a machine that does all his breathing for him. Not sure yet whether he's going to live."

"What happened to him?"

"That's what I'm trying to figure out. Creed took a tumble off Horseshoe Falls three days ago. A witness says he was fighting with a fella and either stumbled or was pushed from the top of the Falls. Creed's daddy says that Creed and Clive were business partners."

Conley laughed. "Business partners? Hell, Clive couldn't run a lemonade stand if his momma made the lemonade and I collected the nickels for him. He was working up at Eastman's in Kingsport, but he got hurt on the job last winter and ain't worked a day since. He ain't been much use to nobody. He's been on disability."

"What kind of injury did he have?" Kade asked.

"Hurt his back. Had to have surgery," Conley said.

"Yet he's well enough to drive all the way to Montana to go hunting." Kade hung that last statement between them like a bloodied sheet.

Conley stood up, alerting Kade that the conversation was finished. "If I hear from Clive, I'll let him know you asked after him."

Kade was not so easily dismissed. "Do you think there's a chance your son had anything to do with the pharmacy shooting?"

Conley walked over to Kade. His eyes were bulging now, his jaw clenched.

"Darlene!" he hollered. She appeared at the door immediately, not even taking the time to slip back on the heels she'd worn to work. "Mr. Mashburn was just leaving. Please escort him out."

"Thank you for the visit," Kade said, offering his hand. Conley didn't take it. Kade put his notebook and pen back into his shirt pocket. When he reached the office door, he turned back to Conley. "I know this has to be hard on you, Chief. I understand that. But, as you have just pointed out, all your efforts to protect him in the past have failed. This isn't going to go well for either of you if you continue down that path."

Darlene could see that her boss was distraught. It wasn't the first time Clive Conley had put his father in distress. "This way, sir," Darlene said to Kade.

"Thanks, ma'am," he said, smiling. "I believe I can find my own way out."

Once Kade left the office, Conley told Darlene to get Vaughnell back on the line.

"Sorry I couldn't take your call earlier. I was tied up. What's going on?"

"Where is Clive?" she asked, not even bothering with a casual greeting.

"Somewhere between here and Montana. Why?"

"I got a feeling something's terribly wrong with him."

"Him and me both, huh? What kind of wrong? He need a checkup too?"

"Bad wrong," she said. "The kind of wrong that can't be undone."

Conley was silent.

"You listening to me?"

"I hear ya," Conley replied.

"Find Clive! Bring him home before it's too late!"

Chapter 22

When Clint awoke Wednesday, it was already mid-morning. Monday evening's flight from Paris had been pleasant enough, other than a moment of wind shear when the plane seemed to drop a few feet. A few women screamed, and one man, who'd had too many drinks, puked all over his own feet. Fortunately, he was sitting far from Clint and Zeb. They'd both slept most of the way to New York City, arriving on Tuesday around 10 a.m. They'd picked up the rental car and headed south for Tennessee.

Zeb was sitting in the dining room of the Hampton Inn reading the Kingsport Times-News when Clint ambled in.

"So sorry," Clint said. "How long have you been here?"

"I was up early enough to see the sun rise over the mountains," Zeb said.

"Before daybreak?" Clint asked, surprised.

Zeb nodded.

Clint pumped out a cup of lukewarm coffee and took a seat across from Zeb. Pockets of loose skin hung underneath Zeb's eyes, evidence of his stress.

"I want to thank you again, Zeb, for accompanying me on this trip. I know there is nothing about it that is easy for you."

Zeb ran his hand across the top of the newspaper, avoided looking at Clint, swallowed hard before speaking.

"I owe it to Burdy," he said, his voice shaky. "It's been a long time since I've seen the sun come up over those mountains. I forgot how much I love these hills in October. Makes me wish I had nothing to do for the next week but wander through them, hunting deer."

"I didn't know you liked to hunt," Clint said.

"Oh, I don't anymore. The war took all that want for hunting outta me. It's being in the woods I miss mostly."

"I bet."

They drank their coffee together, listening to Otis Redding's "Sittin' on the Dock of the Bay" playing softly over the hotel's sound system. When the song finished, the announcer identified the station as WKOS, "Good times, Great oldies." The last time Zeb heard Redding's song, Kade was singing it. Zeb wondered what had become of Kade. Had he gone off to Nashville, become a big star?

Zeb was suddenly keenly aware of how much time he'd spent over the years wondering. He lived in the state of wondering more often than he lived anyplace else. He wondered how life would have been different had the Japs never bombed Pearl Harbor. He wondered how life would have been different if Maizee's momma hadn't died; if her daddy hadn't abandoned her to Doc and Leela-Ma; if Rain hadn't been born; or if he hadn't contracted scarlet fever, hadn't lost his hearing; if Sarge hadn't died in that field; if Zeb hadn't picked up the gun and shot those Germans, that kid; if he hadn't married Maizee at all but headed off to Nashville with Kade instead. God, there was so much about Zeb's life that he wished had gone differently.

"Zeb." Clint paused, then tried again. "Zeb?"

"Sir?" Zeb replied.

"I was saying you look completely lost."

Zeb sat back in his chair and stretched out his legs, his hips sore from the days of travel. "I suppose I am," he said. "This area is known as the Lost State."

"Tennessee?"

"Nah, just a part of Eastern Tennessee."

"I'm confused."

"Well, I've been confused for many years," Zeb replied. Both men chuckled.

"Do we have a plan for today?" Clint asked.

"If you're ready, I say we head to the hollers."

"The hollers?" Clint raised his eyebrows.

"That's native language for 'wide spot in the road,' which is what the community of Christian Bend is. Or was. Who knows? Maybe it's a major metropolis by now. Although, from what I can see of the hotel parking lot, it doesn't look to me like Kingsport has changed all that much. A few more roadways, but it looks like the smokestacks at Eastman are still the tallest features around."

"And once we are in Christian Bend?" Clint asked.

"Lord only knows," Zeb replied. "Hopefully, we'll be able to track down what's become of Burdy. Meet you in the parking lot in ten minutes?"

"Oui," Clint replied.

Zeb folded the newspaper and stuck it under his arm. He didn't bother telling Clint about the article he'd just read concerning a shooting in Bean Station in September, one in which three people had been shot and killed and one woman critically injured—a Mrs. Burdy Luttrell. Police had not yet made an arrest in the case and, according to the updated report, had no leads.

The killer was still on the loose.

Chapter 23

A pair of mourning doves camped outside Burdy's bedroom window woke her shortly after dawn on Wednesday. The male's repetitive coo-coo-cooing stirred her from a deep slumber. She lay there tucked between freshly laundered sheets, thinking about the time she and Clint had woken in a hotel in Paris to find a pair of mourning doves cooing and nesting in a planter box on the balcony.

"Did you know that turtledoves mate for life?" he had asked, wrapping his arm around her shoulders and drawing her to his chest.

"Mmmm, maybe," she answered sleepily.

"They do everything as a pair, always faithful to each other. They build their nest together; they hunt for seeds together; they raise their young together. Even their broods come in pairs."

Burdy shifted, slid one leg between Clint's, and breathed him in. She loved those early morning moments, lying in Clint's arms, the world around them a gentle whisper of activity. Shop owners turning keys in locks to ready their wares for the day. The soft footsteps of another hotel guest in the hall. A motorcycle whirring by the balcony below.

"Like twins, you mean?" she asked.

"Yes, something like that." Clint laughed. "The female almost never lays just one egg. She lays two eggs per brood, and she can do this several times a year."

"I would have liked to had twins," Burdy said.

"Really?" Clint said.

"Well, who knows if I would have really liked it. All that work, but I wish I'd had more than one child. Mind you, Wheedin managed to be the work of half a dozen children all by her lonesome."

Clint laughed again. Burdy loved his rumbling laughter, the way it echoed around her, not like thunder but like the earth moving beneath her, offering her a different vantage point from which to view her surroundings.

"I guess what I mean is that I wish Tibbis had lived a good long life, that we could have made more babies if we wanted."

Clint pulled Burdy closer, kissed the top of her forehead. "I am sorry you were widowed at such a young age. I can't know what that is like, but I can imagine how lost I would be without you in my life. I would be in constant mourning, like the turtledove without his mate. I hate what you have endured, but I am thankful, always, that this loss has brought you to me."

Burdy had climbed atop Clint, kissed him longingly and deeply, straddling him with her legs at his hips. One of the things she loved best about Clint was that he always found it in his heart to honor Tibbis while also acknowledging that, without that loss, the "they" of Burdy and Clint would not exist. They made love that morning against the backdrop of cooing turtledoves and Parisians rising to a new day. It was one of Burdy's favorite memories with Clint: their morning together in that hotel room, awash in light and the love they made.

Now, the cooing outside her bedroom window stopped abruptly, the doves having flown off in search of breakfast. Burdy threw back the chenille cover and sat up. Her pink linen nightgown was bunched up underneath her hips. She stared at her legs and noted the marked difference between them. One was muscular, strong, quite capable still of hiking up to Horseshoe Falls if her lungs could keep up. The other leg, the injured one, was withered like a dry twig that would have been a strong limb had it never been broken off the tree.

She ran her hand along the outer edges of the deep scar forming. It looked like a steep canyon road running the length of her upper thigh. It was still sore but didn't pain her like before.

She reached for a tub of balm on the bedside table. Doc had made it and given it to her with the strict instructions to apply it several times a day. It had helped in the healing a great deal, keeping the skin pliable, preventing it from itching so much.

"I need to thank Doc for this," she thought. "I ought to make him a pie or take him a jar of that blackberry shine I've been hoarding."

She scooped out three fingers full of the balm and rubbed it into her injured leg. Then, still sitting on the side of her bed, she did the stretches the physical therapist had taught her, tucking toes and heels and lifting her leg, repeating the motions again and again. As she moved through the exercises, Burdy recited from her favorite Bible verses.

Reciting Scripture had a way of calming Burdy, helping her center herself and prepare for the day. Whenever Burdy began her day this way, which she did most every day, it put her in the presence of her long-dead auntie. Evoking the spirits of her people equipped Burdy to see the eternal nature of love and time, even when mortal bodies pass on.

Sometimes, while meditating, Burdy had visions. Often they involved Tibbis or Wheedin, one of the men she cared for at Pressmen's, or one of her neighbors. But that Wednesday morning, as she sat on the edge of her bed reciting Psalm 121, oddly enough, she had a vision of Zebulon Hurd. In her vision, Burdy saw Zeb walking up the road, past the big oak in the graveyard where Maizee was buried, past the church. As Zeb moved by the church, he tried to wave off Con Christian, who was erratically running slightly ahead of him and singing loudly: "Then the remnant went to welcome home the brave. The people of God joined alongside the wounded, carrying them. With Zebulon came the lame and the brokenhearted. And God opened the skies and Rain came forth. And the tears came down all around, all around. And the tears came down all around."

"Visions are odd things," Burdy thought as she put away the balm, wiped her hands on a hanky, and lifted herself up from the bed, taking care not to put too much pressure on her bad leg. As she dressed for the day—a purple paisley blouse paired with a pair of her favorite jeans—Burdy recalled the vision she had of Maizee in heaven, the one in which Maizee made her promise to go to France in search of Zeb.

"Some visions, like that one, are meant to be heeded," Burdy told herself.

She slipped on a pair of delicate dragonfly earrings and a matching necklace handcrafted by a New Orleans artist. Wheedin had given them to her for Mother's Day ten years prior. They were Burdy's favorite because Wheedin gifted them, and because when she was a young girl one of the stories Auntie Tay told her concerned dragonflies.

"Whenever you see a dragonfly, pay close attention," Auntie Tay had said. "You are being visited by an ancestor."

"How will I know who it is?" asked Burdy.

"It's not important to know which of your ancestors has come to you," said Auntie Tay. "It's enough to know that they come to you because they love you very much."

From that moment on, whenever Auntie Tay had to take leave of Burdy or Hota, she would pull them close and whisper, "Remember, the dragonfly will always bring you love enough for whatever lies ahead."

In return, Burdy would hug her auntie and reply, "I wish you enough, too."

Those were the last words Burdy spoke to her auntie as Tay lay dying in the front room of her Rogersville home a few months before Wheedin was born. Cousin Hota had been unable to attend

Tay's sickbed because he was living and working in Colorado by then and couldn't get the time off.

Burdy, who was swollen with child, gave her beloved auntie a kiss on the cheek, then said, "Off you go with the dragonflies. I wish you enough." Tay's heart made one last faint knocking beat and stopped. Her final breath was barely more than a whisper.

Tibbis, who had been at Burdy's side throughout those last hours, pulled her close and held her as she wept for the woman who had always been more mother than auntie to Burdy.

The loss was still so immense after all these years that, as Burdy twisted her thick gray hair into a braid, the tears fell. She wiped them away and finished pinning her braid to the nape of her neck.

She looked at her watch. It was nearly 11 a.m. Rain would come by soon. Kade Mashburn had called from Knoxville, said he was headed up to the Bend and wanted to meet with the both of them, ask some questions, said he thought he might have an idea who was responsible for the shooting at Laidlow. And Burdy, for one, was ready to put the whole thing behind her.

Chapter 24

Several days had passed since Thomasina last saw Kade. Between work and worry, she'd lost track of time. She knew he'd been up to the ICU to see one of the patients because a friend who worked that floor told her she'd seen him talking to the patient's family member, an old man with an oxygen tank.

Her pal said the ICU patient had taken a bad tumble off a mountain and struck his head, done some damage to his spinal cord. She wasn't sure if he would live or not, but if he did, he would spend the rest of his days hooked up to a respirator. All Thomasina knew for sure was that Kade's case must be taking place somewhere other than Knoxville.

She'd been by his apartment a few times, watered the plants, kept the Walter Anderson paintings company, and paced the hallway, hoping he would come bursting through the door any minute. She could tell he'd been by there at least once because there were shoes pulled out, messy stacks of t-shirts on the bed, and a few freshly laundered shirts hanging from the closet door. And his shaving kit was missing from the bathroom. She surmised he had been home to pack a bag and taken off again in a hurry. Whatever was going on was tied to the fellow in ICU; that was obvious. Finally, she found a note from Kade on the kitchen counter:

> I'm off to Hawkins County. Working a case. Thinking about you every moment we're apart. I'll call soon as I'm able.
> Later babe,
> Kade

What else could she do except wait and worry and hope he'd call soon?

Kade left Bean Station later than he intended. He'd never been optimistic enough to expect such a lengthy sit-down meeting with Conley. It bothered Kade somewhat that he and the Chief had not parted ways amicably. He had hoped that they would, given their common connections. Still, Kade knew a person couldn't get caught up seeking the approval of others, not if he hoped to do a law enforcement job well.

The crime lab had little evidence to go on, but the information he'd been able to get from Chief Conley had Kade convinced that he was on the right track. His department had been tracking Creed McPheters and Clive Conley for some time.

It was clear that the two were running drugs down to the Florida line, and Creed's daddy had all but confirmed that. But the most helpful bit of information came when the Chief told Kade about Clive's back injury. That was one piece to the puzzle that Kade didn't know. It was one thing to run drugs and quite another to be addicted to them. If what Chief Conley said was true, it seemed that Clive was into smuggling for more than just the extra cash.

As soon as he pulled his Trans Am out of the parking lot, Kade drove south three blocks to Laidlow's Pharmacy. He parked beside the building, got out, and walked to the pay phone across the street, where he made two calls: one to his boss in Knoxville and one to Detective Wiley. He related his conversation with the Chief to his boss and suggested they might want to figure out a way of getting Clive Conley back to Tennessee. He asked Detective Wiley to meet him at Laidlow's.

"I'm about fifteen minutes out if you can wait that long," Wiley said.

"I'll be here," Kade assured him.

Kade knew Wiley to be a straight shooter. He was committed to honoring his oath of office, no matter the personal or professional cost to him. The two men had met a few years earlier when they both served on a task force team for Governor McWherter. Det.

Wiley would call Kade every now and then and ask for help with a case he was working. Kade trusted him. He assumed Det. Wiley felt the same about him.

Kade was standing in the aisle between the cough medicines and the Dr. Scholl's foot gels when Wiley arrived at Laidlow's. They shook hands and exchanged pleasantries, and then Kade asked Wiley if he could walk him through the scene of the shooting. Wiley obliged him.

"Laidlow's is a mom and pop pharmacy, unlike those big marts popping up all over the place," Wiley said as the two walked past the antacids. "See the soda fountain over there?" he nodded to a back corner. "Those stools are full most every day at noon. This is the gathering hole for people in Bean Station. Some of the regulars come in here every day for lunch, for coffee, or just to catch up with each other. The Liar's Club gathers here every day from 10 a.m. to 11."

"The Liar's Club?" Kade wasn't sure he'd heard Wiley right.

"Yeah, you know, the retirees who have nothing better to do than sit around and bitch about how things are now and how much better they were back then." Both men laughed.

"Okay, gotcha."

Wiley stopped halfway down the aisle where the rubber gloves and hydrogen peroxide were shelved. "This is where he killed those people. Right here." Wiley ran his foot over a confetti-inspired linoleum tile.

Kade stared at the floor, imagining the fear of that moment. "Lemme ask you something," he began. "Why do you think the gunman killed those people?"

"Hell if I know," Wiley said. "If killing made sense, more people would do it, I reckon."

"Good point, albeit a troubling thought."

"Listen, Kade, I learned a long time ago to make peace with the fact that I can't know why people do the shit they do. They're crazy. Or I hope that's it, because thinking that a sane person could walk into pharmacy like this and just start slaughtering people is scarier than having a crazy person running around killing folks."

"I knew I liked the way you think," Kade said. The two men walked outside. The sun had disappeared in a haze of afternoon clouds and gathering pollution. A chill shook Kade, but he didn't know if it was from the air or from being in a place visited by evil. "How well do you know Clive Conley?"

Wiley shook his head and kicked at a rock with the tip of his shoe, which hadn't seen black polish since the day he first put it on. "Too well."

"What do you mean?" Kade asked.

Wiley shoved his hands deep in his pockets and said, "Conley and I grew up together. We don't have too many secrets from each other."

"So you knew about Clive's addiction problems?"

"Oh, yeah."

"You sound disgusted about that."

"Just tired of it, I guess. I've had a firsthand seat to all the trauma Clive's put his daddy and momma through."

"And?"

"And what?" Wiley asked. "What is it you want to know about Clive?"

"Do you think he could have been the shooter? Killed those people?"

Wiley turned away from Kade, faced the mountains the sun would be soon slipping behind, and wished that he had gotten out of Bean Station back when he was a young man. He'd thought about going out to Idaho, getting a job with the Forest Service or some whitewater-rafting group. He would have liked that very much. Being out in a place so remote that the only sound was the wind whistling through the trees and the owls hooting at each other. And the only killing was of the deer or elk a man needed for eating. He should have gone. Maybe he still would one day.

"I wish I could tell you differently," Wiley said finally. "But knowing Clive the way I do, I can't." He looked hard at Kade. "I do think he could have done it. He definitely has it in him."

Chapter 25

Rain ran up the dirt drive, past the barn where the hogs were nosing their way through the trough, sucking up each last morsel of the morning's slop. He stopped just short of the front porch, out by the old well, recalling a long-ago moment when, as a young boy, he had tried to crawl into the bucket and lower himself into the cavern's darkness to retrieve a toy truck Doc had bought him.

He must have been six, maybe seven. Leela-Ma, who was feeding the chickens at the back of the house, about had a heart attack when she'd seen him straddling, one foot in the bucket and one on the edge of the well. She threw down the chicken feed and ran at him, grabbed him around the waist, and jerked him to dry ground moments before the bucket broke loose and fell into the water.

Leela-Ma burst into tears from sheer fright, which scared Rain, so he began crying too. When Leela-Ma related the story to Doc over dinner that night they all laughed.

Now Rain wiped away the sweat dripping down his forehead and looked at his watch. It was 9:30. He'd clocked seven miles since leaving the house at 8:15. Not bad, considering the hills and his age. He spit into the grass and the hogs fussed at him.

The back door was open, further sign that Doc was off and about already. Breakfast plates were stacked in the sink, and the coffee pot was empty. Rain poured himself a glass of water, drank it, and then poured himself another.

Leela-Ma walked into the kitchen. Her perfume—Shalimar, always—gave her away. Even as a young boy, Rain could tell when Leela-Ma was in a room because of the sweetness of her presence.

"Oh, Rain, you liked to scared me to death!" Leela-Ma exclaimed. "I had no idea you were here." She brushed her hand over his hair, which was matted in sweat.

"Went for a run," Rain said.

"I can see that." Leela-Ma had on her best pink lipstick and her grey hair was curled. She set her Bible on the table.

"You headed somewhere?"

"Ladies' Bible Study. It's Wednesday, remember?"

"Guess I forgot about Ladies' Bible Study." Rain winked. He leaned against the counter.

"Sit down," Leela-Ma said. "I have some biscuits left over from breakfast." She pulled a bowl from the stove, removed the linen towel that covered it, and then reached behind Rain and pulled out a jar of honey, sat it on the table.

"No, no." Rain shook his head. "I can't. I've got to get home and shower. I'm supposed to meet with Burdy at 11:30."

Leela-Ma put the honey back. "You speaking to Burdy now?"

Rain nodded.

"Good to hear that. Me and Doc have been praying for the two of you. How is she doing?"

"Better every day," Rain said.

"I need to get over there. I have a pound cake in the freezer I've been meaning to get to her. Maybe I'll drop by after Bible study."

"I don't know if that would be such a good time," Rain said. He put his glass in the sink and blew his nose into a paper towel he'd yanked from the roll.

"Why not?" Leela-Ma asked. She put the linen back over the biscuits and set them on the stove.

"Kade called. He wanted to meet with us."

"About what?" Leela looked at her watch and picked up her Bible.

"That accident up at Horseshoe Falls."

154

"Okay." Rain could tell she was concerned but trying not to show it. "Well," she said, "I hate to rush off, but I've got to get going or I'll be late. C'mon, walk me over to the church."

Chapter 26

As Kade turned onto Christian Bend Road, he switched off the Jim Croce song playing on the radio and rolled down the window. He couldn't remember the last time he'd been to the Bend, but it always felt like coming home.

The smoke settling over the mountains that usually burned off by late morning lingered today. He heard gunshots in the distance. Hunters. Kade recalled the time he got his first buck. He and Zeb and the Mosely brothers had made camp at a spot that Shug Mosely told the boys about. Looking back, Kade couldn't believe Ida and Shug had let them go out alone like that. They weren't but fourteen or fifteen years of age.

"You couldn't do that now," Kade thought. "Liable to run into somebody's illegal grow, get into trouble." Looking off toward the river, Kade wondered how many unknown bodies might have been carried off downstream on account of running into the wrong thing at the wrong time.

Rain showered and pulled on a pair of jeans and a flannel shirt of his dad's that still hung in his momma's closet. Back when he graduated from high school, people from the Bend were all the time telling Rain how much he favored his daddy. "Except you got your mama's coloring," they'd add.

Lately, though, people had been telling him how much he looked like Kenny Loggins. One gal had even followed him through the hallways at the UT Medical Center to ask for his autograph. He thought it was a compliment, but he missed people telling him how much he looked like his father. He didn't have any pictures of the older Zeb.

Burdy had her wooden cutting board out and half a dozen Mason jars lined up on the counter when Rain arrived. She was cutting up a root that looked like a white yam. Rain kissed the top of her head and gave her a hug.

"Didn't nobody teach you to be careful around a woman with a knife?" Burdy scolded.

Ignoring her admonishment, Rain blurted out, "Do you think I look like my dad?"

Burdy set the knife on the cutting board, took a long look at Rain. "When you was a boy, you favored Maizee, but once puberty hit, you began to look more like your daddy. By the time you got to high school, you and him could've been twins. But now, you are just a good mix of them both. You got your momma's coloring and your daddy's build."

"I never got to see him at this age," Rain said. "He's younger in all the family pictures. Did you take any pictures of him when you were in France? If you did, could I see them?"

Burdy picked up her knife again and chopped up the root, filling the jars until every one was packed full. She had one root left. The entire kitchen smelled of ginger. When she was done, Burdy wiped off her knife until it shone, and then she turned back to Rain.

"I might have a picture or two of him somewhere. You sure you want to see?"

"Yes." Rain could see the worry cloud Burdy's aqua eyes. "Wouldn't you want to know if you were me?"

"I suppose," she said, pointing at a cane hanging on the back of one of the dining room chairs. "Hand me that."

Rain did as he was instructed.

"It's just that I don't know what's the good of all this." She began walking toward the extra bedroom where she kept the cupboard for her roots. Suddenly she stopped in the living room and turned back toward him. "You coming?"

"Where we going?"

"Bring me those jars, would you?"

"Do you want me to put the lids on them?"

"No," she said. "They need to dry out."

Rain carried an armful of jars into the dark room and went back for the rest. Burdy lined them up on the shelf next to a variety of other jars with herbs drying.

"Can you reach that box way up there?" she finally asked, pointing to a white box at the top of the cupboard.

Rain reached up and pulled the box down. "This shoebox?"

"Yeah," she said. "Carry it back to the kitchen for me."

Kade pulled up alongside the mailbox marked "Luttrell." He rolled the window closed, turned the ignition off, and looked in the mirror, straightening his wind-blown hair. He couldn't explain it, but something left him feeling catawampus. He sat in the car for a moment trying to sort out what was making him feel so anxious.

Maybe it was because he knew these people, whereas, most of the time he didn't know those he had to question. The Bend was the community of his youth. He felt more protective of Burdy and Rain than of people he didn't know. Most of the time, Kade was dealing with people he had never met and might never meet again. But these people in the Bend were his people.

Inhaling deeply, Kade did something he hadn't done in a very long time—he prayed. Sort of. "Help me get this right, Maizee," he said. Ever since she died, Kade had felt like he had a direct line to heaven.

People in Tennessee was always talking about the kin who went on before them, who were watching out over them. For Kade, Maizee was that kin. Even though they weren't blood kin, they were kindred in their spirits, and that had always been enough for Kade.

He locked the car and walked up to the porch, smiling at the yellow mums growing alongside the walk. Burdy always could coax beauty from the earth. It was her way.

"Come on in," Burdy called from the kitchen in response to Kade's knocking. "We're back here." Kade opened the screen door and walked in to an overwhelming smell of some spice. It had been years since he'd entered this house. Walking through it now felt like time traveling. The doilies on the end tables, the embroidered footstool next to the davenport, the braided rug over the shiny oak floors—it all looked the same as it always had. Even Burdy looked much the same as she always had.

"I think I'm the only thing around here that's aged," Kade said. He was standing in the doorway between the kitchen and the living room.

Rain and Burdy were sitting at the table, a shoebox between them. They were shuffling through a stack of photographs spread out all across the table.

"What's that smell?" Kade asked.

"Some of Burdy's witching root," Rain replied.

"Ginger," Burdy said.

"Lord, that is strong stuff." Kade walked over to Burdy and stood behind her, squeezing her shoulders. Speaking to Rain, he signed, "It's sure good to see you again, buddy."

"You don't have to sign," Rain said. He pointed to his hearing aid. "They keep making these better and better."

"The miracle of modern medicine," Kade said.

"Something like that."

Kade walked over and tousled Rain's hair. "What's a fellow have to do to get a hug from you? Or are you too grown up for all that stuff?"

Rain carefully placed the photos on the table, then stood up and gave Kade a proper bear hug. The two men were equal in height now, able to stand eye to eye.

"Did I interrupt your morning decoupage class?" Kade teased.

"Not exactly," Burdy said. "We are searching for something."

159

Kade picked up a photo from the pile and stared at it. "This looks like the Eiffel Tower."

"That's because it is the Eiffel Tower," Burdy replied matter-of-factly.

"But I could swear that's you standing in front of it."

"That's because it is me standing in front of it."

"You went to Paris? You?"

"Don't act so surprised," Burdy scolded. She did not look up and did not pause her searching, continuing to shuffle through each photograph. "I am much more well traveled than you would imagine."

"Are you now?" Kade smiled at Rain. "Did you know that Burdy was such a world traveler? Has she been up to Rhode Island to see you?"

Rain shook his head. "No. I had no idea until just the other day. I figured Burdy for someone who had never left Hawkins or Sullivan counties."

"Well, you figured me wrong, didn't you?"

"Apparently so," Kade said. He pulled out a chair and sat between the two. "Who is this dapper-looking fellow you are with? The tour guide?"

"No!" Burdy snapped. She did not appreciate Kade's inference that she was too backwards and too uneducated to travel. She'd probably seen more of the world than Kade. In fact, she was sure of it. "That's a friend of mine from France."

"What sort of friend?" Kade asked, winking at Rain.

"A very good one." Burdy's tone made it clear that they were done discussing her business.

"I bet," Kade replied.

Burdy ignored his impertinent remark. "I'm sure you didn't come all the way out here to talk about my adventures overseas."

"I might have had I known about them," Kade said. He wasn't ready to let go of the amusing notion of Burdy traveling to France. Kade had always been a tease. "What exactly are you searching for?"

"It's not what, it's who," Rain replied. He was studying each photo he happened upon, scanning each face.

"Okay," Kade said. "Who are you searching for?"

"That's for me to know and you to find out," Burdy replied smartly. She wasn't giving up any further information. "You'll need a subpoena before I answer any more questions."

Kade raised both hands in the air. "Okay, okay. I was only kidding. I didn't mean to offend you. You know I love you, Burdy."

"You better be careful, Kade. She might put a hex on you. Or make one of them voodoo dolls in your likeness," Rain teased.

"Boys. You can't kill them and they refuse to grow up," Burdy interjected.

"Boys?" Kade asked. "Now that I'm sixty, I'm dang near a senior citizen."

"You are, aren't you?" Burdy said. Now it was her turn to poke fun. "Although you don't act your age and never will, I suppose."

"Which reminds me, a friend of yours sends her love."

"Who is that?"

"Thomasina."

"Kade Mashburn! Are you seeing Thomasina?"

"I've seen more of her than you have, I'd wager." Kade laughed and elbowed Rain, who joined him laughing.

"Nice comeback," Rain said. "Touché."

"Thanks. Being a smartass is a skill I'm still honing."

"You better treat that woman, right, Kade. Or I will put a hex on you. One that will shrivel up your manhood overnight," Burdy said. "And that's not a threat. That's a promise."

Kade threw up his hands in surrender again. "No worries. I like this one. A lot. Besides, Thomasina can take pretty good care of herself."

"She's had to," Burdy said.

"Yes, I know," Kade replied.

The phone rang. Burdy put the photos down, glared at the two men as if daring them to answer her own phone, and grabbed her cane. Steadying herself, she rose slowly from the chair and walked out to the living room, picking up the phone on the fifth ring.

"So what exactly are you two looking for?" Kade asked Rain when she left.

"You really want to know?"

"Yes."

"A recent photo of my dad."

"Your dad?" Kade asked. He didn't understand. "Why would Burdy have pictures of your dad?"

"It's a long, convoluted story," Rain replied.

Burdy was back, looking disgruntled. "It's a call for you, Kade."

"For me? Who would be calling me here?"

"He said he was your boss. He also said it was urgent that he speak with you."

Chapter 27

Burdy could hear Kade from the other room. She could tell from his tone that something troubling had happened, but she couldn't make out any full sentences. An "Oh my god" and a couple of swear words that had never been uttered in her home and even an "I can't believe it," but nothing clear. She and Rain continued their search.

"Where is this?" Rain asked. He held up a beach photo.

"Lemme see," Burdy said. Rain handed her the photo. "Oh, that's at Arromanches. At Normandy. Where they brought all the equipment and supplies in during the war."

"Why are there so many people on the beach?"

Burdy handed the photo back to Rain. "It was an art thing. They were marking the numbers of bodies in the sand, the ones of those who died during the invasion."

Rain peered at the photo, now noticing the outlines of bodies. There wasn't a square inch of space between them. "Unbelievable," he said, shaking his head.

"Yes." Burdy nodded. "Numbers don't register but bodies do."

Kade came back into the room, his face white as cotton. He looked like he might puke. Rain pushed his seat back and went over to his friend.

"You okay? What's the matter?"

"Get him a glass of water," Burdy instructed. "Sit down, Kade." She pushed out a chair with her good foot.

Kade sat and drank the water Rain offered him.

Rain sat back down as Kade shook his head. His hands were trembling. "I knew I had a bad feeling about today." He took a few more gulps of water, then cupped his hands around the glass and continued to hold it in his lap, as if he needed something to hang on to, to steady himself.

"That was Detective Wiley calling to tell me that they found Chief Conley's son dead."

"What?" Rain exclaimed.

"Clive? Dead where?" Burdy asked.

"Laramie."

"Laramie, Wyoming? What was he doing out there?" Rain asked.

"I met with Conley yesterday. He said Clive was headed out to Montana for a hunting trip." Kade's shoulders drooped. He took another sip of water. "But I suspected it was something more than just a casual hunting trip."

"I don't understand," Burdy said. She pulled a hanky from her bra, wiped her eyes and her mouth, then stuffed it back into her bra.

"Well, Clive is what I came out here to talk to you about," Kade said. "I suspect he might have been the one who killed those people at Laidlow's. Shot you. And I'd bet the farm that he's the one who was fighting with Creed McPheeters that day you were up at Horseshoe Falls, Rain."

"My lands!" Burdy said. "The Chief's son?"

"Yeah," Kade said.

"What makes you think he was the one fighting with Creed?" Rain asked.

"They were business partners of sorts. Creed's daddy confirmed that they had a sizable grow up on his property. Our agency has been tracking them for some time now. We know they were running stuff through Georgia, into Florida."

"So you think Clive meant to kill Creed that day, pushing him from the cliff?" Rain asked.

"I don't know," Kade said. "That's what I was hoping you could tell me. Was Creed pushed or did he stumble off that ledge?"

Rain thought back to that day, recalling his moment of indecision when he couldn't decide whether to intervene or not, when he didn't know that Creed was one of the men up on the ledge. What had his hesitation cost Creed?

"I'm not sure whether he was pushed or not," Rain said. "But if that was Clive as you say, he was giving Creed a pretty good licking."

"Tell me what you saw," Kade said. He put down the glass and took out a tape recorder, clicked it on.

"Well, I've told all this to the deputies who came out that day," Rain said. "They were fighting pretty close to the edge. The bigger of the fellas had his hands around Creed's neck. He was throttling him, obviously enraged. I started running for them when Creed came flying off the cliff. I didn't know it was Creed until he hit the water." Rain shut his eyes as he spoke, seeing it all unfold before him again in slow motion.

"I pulled him out right away and did my best to help him. I should have done more. I wish I had acted sooner to break up the fight."

"How did he die?" Burdy interrupted. Both men looked at her.

"Clive, you mean?" Kade asked.

"Yeah," she said. "How'd he die?

"A screwdriver."

Rain scrunched up his face. "A screwdriver?"

"Yeah. Police got a report of a break-in at a dentist office there in Laramie. When they arrived they found him slumped over in a corner of an office, blood everywhere. He'd stabbed himself. Over twenty-six times to the head, driving that screwdriver deep into his skull."

"Oh my god!" Burdy exclaimed.

"Dang." Rain sighed. "Can a person really do that to himself?"

Kade nodded. "Addicted people do shit you'd never believe when they are tripping."

"A screwdriver, though," Burdy said. Her brow was knitted in disbelief. "You'd have to be crazy to stab yourself that way."

"How do they know somebody else didn't do it to him?" Rain asked.

"Well the investigation is ongoing, of course. But the doors to the office were locked when they arrived and there were no bloody footprints or blood of any kind leading from the office. Looks like Clive broke in to get at the drugs. They'll do a toxicology test, of course, but I suspect it'll come back with more than one drug in his system."

"So is that why you think he's the one that did the shooting at Laidlow's?" Burdy asked.

"Yeah. He wasn't just in the drug-smuggling business. He was an addict. Chief Conley told me his boy has been in and out of re-hab for years."

"Tragic," Burdy said.

"Damn," Rain said again. "And I thought Momma chose a pretty gruesome way to kill herself."

There was a loud knocking on the door before either Kade or Burdy could respond to Rain's troubling statement.

Chapter 28

Zeb did the driving, pointing out areas of interest as he and Clint made their way through Kingsport. As they drove past Eastman's smokestacks, Zeb told Clint about the lynching of Mary the Elephant.

"God, how awful," Clint said.

"Yes," Zeb said. "People can do the most horrible things all the while convinced they are doing right."

"Don't we both know the truth of that?" Clint replied.

Zeb grew quiet. He wished he hadn't brought up the story of Mary. He'd grown up hearing that story all his life and wondering how people could be so cruel to an innocent animal. But that was back before Pearl Harbor, before Normandy, before his own inconceivable wrongs.

Zeb had come to understand that when military leaders say war is hell, it isn't the battlefield they are referring to. It's the eternal afterward, when a man has to live with what he's done. The killings. The loss of life and limb and buddy and, in Zeb's case, a child. Some men are able to justify wars at any cost. Most, however, struggle through the rest of their lives, trying to reconcile all that the war demanded from them. Zeb fell into the latter category. Even eternity wasn't long enough to work through all that World War II had exacted from him. He'd lost himself and all that he held dear, and coming home this way made all the loss painfully near. He swiped a tear that fell beneath his sunglasses.

"You okay?" Clint asked.

Zeb didn't respond as he turned on the left blinker and he eased the car up to a red light.

"You are awfully quiet all of a sudden."

"Not much to say," Zeb said. His voice cracked.

They rode the rest of the way to Christian Bend in silence, save for the radio. When James Taylor's "You've Got a Friend" came over the airwaves, Clint leaned over and turned it up.

Friendship, Clint mused, is a give and take of sitting with each other in darkness. Zeb's decision to help Clint find Burdy came at great personal cost. Clint couldn't imagine the inner turmoil afflicting Zeb, but he appreciated that Zeb was willing to endure it all because of the distress Clint had been in over Burdy.

Zeb kept saying he owed it to Burdy, which surely was true, but Clint suspected there was a part of Zeb that wanted to come home, had wanted to for a very long time. Burdy's being missing was the lure, but there was something deeper driving him.

When he turned onto Christian Bend Road, a rush of emotion came over Zeb. He felt sick to his stomach. He had an urge to shit. He didn't know whether to keep driving or pull the car over. He rolled down the window, breathed in the mud of the river and the newly mown hayfield.

Clint switched off the radio.

"Mind if we stop here?" Zeb said, pulling the car off to the right, to the parking lot of a boat-loading dock.

"Not at all," Clint said. "I'd like to stretch my legs a bit."

Zeb pulled into a space facing the river. "I'll be back." He headed for the public bathroom.

Clint walked down to the edge of the lot, looked out over the Holston. There were a couple fellows in a boat, trolling, and on downriver a fellow in waders looking for the perfect place to cast. Clint couldn't get over the beauty of the Bend. The trees were flaming red and glittering gold. The Holston, polished silver.

"This place looks like God's treasure chest," Clint said when Zeb returned.

"It does, doesn't it?" Zeb replied. "When a person grows up here, they can do without a lot of things but not without beauty. It's one of God's character traits, you know. Beauty is."

"To behold the beauty of the Lord," Clint said.

"Glory and beauty are in his presence," Zeb replied.

They walked back to the car. Before getting in, Zeb glanced one more time at the riverbed. Was this the place Doc found Maizee? Or was it on upriver? Silently, he prayed, "I am so, so sorry, Maizee. I'm sorry." He swiped away a couple more tears as he pulled his sunglasses from atop his head. A blue dragonfly flittered by, its translucent wings dazzling Zeb momentarily.

As he pulled out of the parking lot, Zeb ran his plan by Clint. "We could go by the church and see if the pastor there knows anything. If something bad has happened to Burdy, he'd be the one to know. I mean if she's in the hospital or you know…"

"The graveyard?" Clint replied.

"Yeah."

"You have another plan? One that doesn't include Burdy maimed or dead?"

"Well, I mean, we could go by the house first."

Clint had called Burdy's number before they'd left the hotel, but he'd gotten a busy signal. He'd done everything he knew to do to get in touch with her before coming to the Bend. He realized that fear was filling the pit of his stomach now, and he sympathized with Zeb even more.

"It could be that her phone is out of order," Zeb said. "The phone service in the Bend isn't the most reliable."

"Or maybe she's using it?"

"Maybe." Zeb didn't want to get Clint's hopes up too high.

They settled for going by Burdy's house first, for no other reason than neither man wanted to hear bad news. If Burdy was dead, they wanted to postpone that news as long as possible. If she was hospitalized, there was hope.

The one thing neither of them had counted on was that Burdy herself might greet them. If the thought had occurred to either of them that Burdy might be at her house, healthy and whole, they might not have made the long trip over deep waters, because it would surely mean something worse than death. It would mean Burdy didn't want anything to do with Clint. That after all these years, she was done with him.

Chapter 29

Burdy walked out of the room to see who was knocking at the front door, Rain called after her, "Is this him?" He walked over and held out a picture. In it a man sat leaning against a stone half-wall. Behind him was the old wooden mill wheel churning water.

Burdy looked at it. "Yep, that's the one. And that's the river Aure. That's right near where he lives. I took that four or five years ago. I can't remember." She handed the photo back. Whoever was on the porch knocked again. "Yes, that's your dad."

Rain walked back into the kitchen, staring at the photo.

"Can I see?" Kade asked.

Rain handed him the picture.

Kade studied it. "Man, you really do look like your dad."

"Good-looking fella, ain't he?" Rain said, grinning.

Then both of them heard a shout from the other room. "OH MY GOD! CLINT!"

Rain and Kade almost fell over each other scrambling to get a look at Burdy's Frenchman.

Clint stood in the doorway, hat in one hand, cane in the other. And realized that his worst fear was true: Burdy hadn't been answering his calls because she didn't want anything to do with him.

"I'm sorry," he said quietly. "This was a mistake." He started to back up, stepping on the toes of whoever was standing behind him.

"A mistake?" Burdy asked. "What are you doing here?"

"I should leave. I've shouldn't have come. I'm sorry." He turned to go, and Zeb moved to the side, out of sight of the door.

"Hold on just a minute!" Burdy grabbed Clint's coattails. "Wait! There's been a misunderstanding. I was in the hospital."

Clint froze. He turned back around, stepped just over the doorsill. "You were in the hospital? What happened? Why didn't you call me? I was worried. I was sick with worry. I thought you might be dead." Clint grabbed Burdy and pulled her to him. He kissed her, long and passionately. She kissed him back, just as long, just as energetically. Both their canes fell to the floor.

Kade and Rain watched, gap-mouthed, from the doorway separating the two rooms. They'd never considered Burdy as anything but asexual. They snickered at each other like two frat boys, watching Burdy kiss a man the way a woman in love does, oblivious to anything or anyone.

And then Zeb stepped back into view, standing between the front door and the screen door he was holding.

Rain saw him before he saw Rain.

"Dad?"

"Rain?" Zeb said. He slipped around the two lovers, stepping over both canes. But then he froze. Did Rain even want to see him? Zeb stood there, sobbing unabashed, unsure of whether to turn and run back to France or run to Rain. He could not move.

So Rain did. Pushing Kade aside, Rain went to his father, nearly knocking him over, but then picking him up into the kind of bear hug he'd dreamt of giving his dad his whole life long.

Kade, gobsmacked, watched the reunions from the doorway, crying like a repentant man at the altar.

Chapter 30

That first week after Clint and Zeb arrived in the Bend, Clint drove with Burdy up to South Carolina to meet Wheedin. Clint didn't press Burdy for details about everything that happened, deciding he'd let her offer them as she needed. And she certainly did. She talked all the way to South Carolina, reliving every gruesome detail of the shooting, Creed's accident, and Clive's suicide. Clint knew the talking was good therapy, but sometimes, especially when she got to screwdriver part, he wanted to listen to the oldies station in quiet again.

The night prior, Burdy had insisted on packing up the car before supper. Clint had thought that a bit excessive, given that she'd already told him Wheedin's wasn't all that far, about half-a-day's drive away. But Burdy had peculiar ways about her, and Clint knew better than to try and dissuade her. He carried out her overnight bag and sat it on the backseat, just like Burdy instructed. When Clint said he was concerned that somebody might try to steal it, Burdy dismissed his worries with a wave of the hand.

"If they want to steal a bag of granny underwear, let 'em. They'll be sorely disappointed." She laughed.

"They'll probably be confused," Clint said. "Might even think they're an exotic flag from a foreign nation."

Burdy cut him a look that said she didn't think his teasing was all that funny. Clint grabbed her about the waist and started slowly waltzing her across the front porch. The air smelled of honeysuckle. A bashful moon poked its head out over the hills.

They danced slowly, suspended between the luminescence of a setting sun and rising moon. Burdy, her head pressed against Clint's chest, listened to its echoing thrum.

"Such a good and steady heart," she said, looking up at him. He leaned in and kissed her. His lips were warm and wet and gave her chicken skin all over.

They had stopped swaying, were just pressing into each other, finding comfort in the familiar jetties of hips and breasts. Burdy didn't worry about whether Con Christian or Ida Mosely or even Doc and Leela-Ma were headed up Christian Bend Road right that very minute. All that mattered was that she was in Clint's arms again, safe, whole, and wholly loved.

"Marry me," she said.

Clint had asked her dozens of times. This was the first time she'd ever asked him. Her hands were sweating. Her heart was pounding. This—this asking—was much more difficult than Burdy ever imagined. Or maybe it was the waiting part. It had never occurred to her before the vulnerability inherent in such a question.

"Are you serious?" Clint pulled her out to arm's length so he could study her face for any sign of mockery.

"Serious as a heart attack." She laughed again, and her beautiful white hair fell about her shoulders like a veil.

"You trying to give me one?" Clint asked. "But wait! We can't get married. We can't even get engaged. I don't have a ring!"

"You have a pocketknife?"

"A pocketknife?" Clint began to pat his jacket pockets, his pants. "Here." He handed her a small red knife. Burdy took the knife and walked out into the yard, where she cut a six-inch stalk of sedge. She gave Clint the knife and the sedge.

"What am I supposed to do with this?"

"It's my ring," she replied. "Put it on." She held out her hand.

Clint cupped her hand and began to wrap the brown grass gently around her wedding finger, careful not to twist it too tightly.

"I do," Clint replied. "I mean, Oui! Oui! Of course, I'll marry you. I've been waiting a very long time to marry you, Burdy Luttrell." Taking both her hands into his, Clint pulled them to his lips and kissed her grass ring.

While Burdy and Clint made their short journey east to South Carolina, Zeb and his son took a long journey east over the ocean. When Clint and Zeb had made their trip to the Bend, neither of them had imagined they'd stay very long. They had tickets to return to Bayeux. But the visit changed everything, and Clint assigned his ticket to Rain and sent him off with Zeb to collect some things he would need until he and Burdy returned to France, where they would live part of each year, alternating with time living in the Bend.

As Rain took that trip with his dad, all the anger and bitterness he had endured as a child, over the death of his mother and what he thought was the death of his father, began to fall away.

On the drive up to New York to the airport, Rain and Zeb had many long talks. It was painful at times, especially when they spoke of Maizee, but they didn't shy away from the hurts. They had both spent too many years longing for the opportunity to talk about the hard things together.

"I was wrong to abandon you," Zeb said. "I can't explain why I did what I did. I can only tell you that I thought you were better off without me."

Rain couldn't tell his dad it was okay, because it wasn't. Not for any reason. But forgiveness is a choice, and Rain knew that the choice was his to make.

Honestly, he'd forgiven his dad the second Burdy told him what happened on the battlefield, the reason Zeb felt too unworthy to return home. As a child who'd grown up with a disability, Rain knew how feeling worthless makes a person withdraw from the world. He might not understand the guilt a soldier feels long after a war ends, but he knew firsthand the illogical shame of being deaf in a hearing world. He realized that both kinds of loss could lead a person to the same kind of isolation that drove his mentally ill mother to take her own life. Rain hated the thought of anyone he knew feeling the aloneness of guilt and shame, deserved or not.

The two men shared many things on their trip, but it wasn't until Zeb and Rain strolled among the white marble crosses at the American Cemetery at Normandy that Zeb told his son what he'd told Burdy all those years prior, about how he'd killed that young French boy.

"It's okay, Dad. I forgive you," Rain said, hugging Zeb. "I forgive you."

Those words healed a deep brokenness in Zeb. To be forgiven that way, especially by the son he'd done wrong, was a grace Zeb had not expected. He had always hoped for such a grace, always prayed for it, but when Rain finally extended that forgiveness, Zeb had no words. Only tears of relief and gratitude and that always present feeling that he didn't deserve it.

While the others took their journeys, Kade went back to Knoxville, where he helped Boog McPheters plan a funeral for Creed, who had died that Friday after Boog signed the release to have his son removed from the respirator he'd been on since breaking his neck. Kade exchanged notes with Detective Wiley and learned that Clive Conley had written a suicide note before taking the screwdriver to his head. In the note, Clive confessed to the killings at Laidlow and to pushing Creed from the cliff. The suicide had broken Chief Conley. He resigned the day after he learned of his son's death, turning everything over to Wiley.

After he got everything situated with Boog, Kade went to his favorite jewelers and bought a gorgeous engagement ring. Then he went straight to the UT Medical Center and, after bribing the front desk clerk, made a request over the hospital's intercom system: "Thomasina Woodson, this is Kade Mashburn. I am desperately in love with you and I want to know: Will you marry me? If so, meet me down here at the front entrance. I have a little something for you."

Thomasina, who was in the bathroom flushing a bedpan at the time, nearly missed the proposal, but as soon as she walked back into the patient's room, she heard "desperately in love with you" and recognized Kade's voice. The entire floor, nurses and doctors, patients and volunteers, cheered her onto the elevator, where another group of people applauded and urged her to "Hurry before he changes his mind."

Three weeks later, on November 11, Veterans Day, the Kingsport Times-News sent a reporter and a photographer out to Christian Bend to cover the story behind the double wedding of Kade and Thomasina Mashburn and Clint and Burdy Luttrell. Clint decided he'd take Burdy's name as a way of honoring Tibbis and Wheedin.

"Besides," Clint told the reporter, "Burdy informed me that even after we're married, people in the Bend will always refer to her as the Widow Luttrell, so why fight traditions? When you've had the kind of romance we've had, you don't sweat the small stuff. I'm just thankful we both lived to see this day. I'm honored to take her name and I'm grateful she'll have an old man like me."

It had all been Kade's idea, the notion of a double wedding, although he'd warned Preacher Blount that he didn't have a very good track record when it came to marrying.

"Neither do I," Thomasina had interjected.

Preacher Blount, who came out of retirement to perform the ceremony, had never married a divorced person before, much less two of them to each other. He had to sit with the Word of God for a long time figuring it out, but he finally came away with the decision that it wasn't his to figure out. His job was to love people right where they were at, the way God had loved him. The way God loved everybody. God could figure out the details.

Leela-Ma and Doc paid for the wedding. Their gift to the couples. They insisted. Leela worked with the women of the church on all the decorations and the reception, which was held at the new community center up the road a piece.

Wheedin, who couldn't get away any earlier on account of having taken so much time off work already, drove in on Tuesday and had to leave directly after the reception. She wasn't happy that her momma had lied to her all those years about her travels. She couldn't believe Burdy had gone to France without her. "What kind of momma does that?" Wheedin asked one of her coworkers, who shrugged off the question, knowing she was just blowing off steam. But Wheedin couldn't help liking Clint. Such a gentleman, and that accent. "Can you find me one like him?" Wheedin asked her momma.

Rain and Zeb stood in as best men—Rain for Kade, Zeb for Clint. Burdy had asked Zeb if he would wear his dress uniform since the wedding was on Veterans Day.

"I don't know about that," Zeb had said. "I don't think that would be right. I haven't worn any uniform since I came off that battlefield." But Rain convinced his dad otherwise.

After he agreed, decorating for the wedding was almost too easy. The church ladies lined the aisles with mini-flags—alternating one American, then one French—hanging them in tiny clear vases from every pew. They rolled white paper over the red carpet and sprinkled red rose petals over the top of it. Ida Mosely made two large arrangements with red roses and white hydrangeas for the front of the church. White candles burned softly all around the baptismal.

The invitations, which Leela sent out because Burdy and Thomasina were too overwhelmed, requested every man and woman who'd ever served in the military to wear their dress uniforms to the wedding. By the time all the guests were seated for the four o'clock ceremony, every single branch of the U.S. Armed Forces was in attendance.

"We've got more soldiers here than Fort Bragg does," the Times-News photographer told the reporter. He lifted his camera to snap a picture of Rain and Zeb escorting Leela and Wheedin down the aisle.

Clint, dressed in his French uniform, and Kade, dressed in a black suit, looked appropriately nervous as the organist struck up the wedding march.

"Remember to breathe and don't lock your knees," Preacher Blount teased. "We only give mouth-to-mouth resuscitation to women at this altar."

Kade bent his knees.

"My knees are permanently bent already," Clint replied.

Preacher Blount chuckled, which put them all at ease.

Thomasina walked in first on Rain's arm, followed by Burdy on Zeb's. Both women were resplendent in navy blue, Thomasina in a designer silk with a train and Burdy in a chiffon with an attached shawl. Both women carried bouquets of white roses and wore smiles that would have lit up Paris. Wheedin and Leela-Ma wept, while Thomasina's sons rolled their eyes and grinned at them.

"Who gives these women away?" Preacher Blount asked.

"With our blessing and all our love, the people of Christian Bend," replied Zeb and Rain in unison.

Preacher Blount moved through the service as he had done hundreds of times before, reciting from the First Epistle to the Corinthians, praying tenderly over each couple, and asking for God's protection and guidance in their lives, stopping short of mentioning the blessing of children, and instead praying for continued good health. Each couple exchanged vows and rings, and then Preacher Blount announced that Kade had chosen a special song to sing.

Rain handed Kade his guitar. As he strapped it on, Kade said, "This isn't your typical wedding song, but it is a love song. And I'd like to dedicate it to my good friend Zebulon Hurd, to all of you who have served this country, whether here or abroad, and to your loved ones. Because if it weren't for you and for the sacrifices you have made on behalf of my wife—she is my wife now, right, Preacher?" Kade paused.

"Almost son, almost," Preacher Blount said. "There is that matter of a kiss to come."

"Oh, yeah," Kade said. "That's the most important part." The congregation laughed. "Anyway, like I was saying, if not for you servicemen and women, days like today might not happen. I live my life every day, thankful for each of you. So this song is my way of thanking you." Then Kade began strumming and singing:

From the lakes of Minnesota
To the hills of Tennessee
Across the plains of Texas
From sea to shining sea…
God bless the U.S.A.

When he finished the last note, there wasn't a dry eye in the church. "I have one more request before I turn the microphone back to Preacher Blount for that all-important kiss." Kade winked at Thomasina, who winked back at him. "Will all of you in uniform please stand?"

All over the church, men and women stood, in dress blues, khakis, greens and whites, some sporting Eisenhower jackets, others wearing their distinctive First Cavalry hats.

Putting his guitar aside, Kade said, "Zeb, come on over here would you, buddy?"

Reluctantly, Zeb joined Kade, who put one arm around his shoulder and shook his hand with the other. "All of us here have waited a long time for this moment. It's a day we thought might never come. So I just want to say it in front of God and everybody: Welcome home, buddy. Welcome home to you all."

Through eyes clouded with tears, Rain looked out over the congregation, who had broken out in applause, and he saw her there, on the third pew back, wearing a red dress. All alone but smiling. It had been years, but Rain would have recognized Mary Esther in a sea of people in Manhattan. He smiled and gave a little wave. She smiled and waved back.

Epilogue

A few months later, Zeb was back home in Bayeux. He and Rain had promised to keep in touch via letters and phone calls. Zeb sat with Father Thom over coffee and croissants and reflected on the enormous changes wrought in his life. He still felt he didn't deserve any of it and said so.

"If you deserved it, it wouldn't be grace, now would it?" Father Thom said in his quiet, assuring way.

"I suppose not," Zeb replied.

"What's your plan for the future?" Father Thom asked. "Will you stay here or move back home?"

"This is my home now," Zeb said. "I will work something out. The house Maizee and I lived in on the property is still there. Burdy said I could come stay in it anytime I want. I may go there to stay from time to time, but I could never move back. There are too many painful memories."

"Yes," Father Thom said. "I understand that. What about Rain? What does he say about this?"

"He says he looks forward to getting to see more of France," Zeb said, smiling. "He's making a list of all the places he wants me to take him."

Father Thom laughed. "God is so good, isn't he?"

"He is," Zeb replied. "He really is."

—THE END—

Author's Note

Christian Bend is the place where I spent much of my time in summer of 1966, after my father was killed in Vietnam. My widowed mother, only twenty-nine, was in such shock, and coping with three children was, understandably, overwhelmed. For an escape, she would leave my brother and me with our great-aunt, Lucille Shropshire Christian. Or, as she was known to most everyone at the Bend, "Cil."

Cil and her deaf stepson, Lon, lived in an old farmhouse on a wide corner. The barn and the house are still standing. My aunt is buried in the church graveyard. On a visit to the church a few years ago, Pat Christian invited me up to her home to see a baby blanket my aunt had made for her son. It was in pristine condition, and I wept as I ran my fingers over it. That quilt, so lovingly made, connected me to a woman who first taught me the importance of story. Every day that summer of '66, we would sit on Cil's front porch, calling to neighbors who passed by, drinking cool water from the well, as Cil told us stories. I say, "Words Rise Up Out of the Country" because these three books—*Mother of Rain*, *Burdy*, and *Christian Bend*—come from a place deep within me. These are, in many ways, the stories of my own life. I hope they resonate with you, the reader, because you are the reason I write. I am forever grateful that you make space for me and my stories in your life. It's good to sit with you a spell.

Of course, none of these stories would be possible without the devotion and expertise of the indefatigable staff of Mercer University Press—Marsha Luttrell (no relation to Burdy), Mary Beth Kosowski, and Jenny Toole. You all really are goddesses. Twenty years ago, Marc Jolley took a risk on publishing my very first book—*Benched: The Memoirs of Judge Rufe McCombs*. It is rare in this business for relationships between writers and publishers to last this long. That Marc still finds my work worthy of publishing both humbles me and makes me proud.

Kelley Land, my weaknesses are your strengths. Thank you for adding the sparkle and making these stories shine.

To my band of early readers—family and friends—your insights and suggestions are invaluable. Thank you.

To Leigh Anne Hoover, my sister storyteller, you bring such light to the world.

To my veteran friends, and veterans everywhere, thank you for your service. You inspired the story of Zebulon Hurd. Welcome home.

To my Uncle Raymond "Doug" Spears and his book-loving wife, Annis, thank you for giving me a home to come back to. And for the firefly show. That was really something.

To Mama and Daddy, with great love for you and all our Appalachian mountain ways.

And thank you, sweet family, for making our story more thrilling than a ride at Dollywood.

Author's Bio

Author Karen Spears Zacharias is a Georgia-raised Gold Star daughter whose work has been featured in the *New York Times*, CNN, National Public Radio, and Good Morning America.

Her 2013 novel, *Mother of Rain* (Mercer), received the Weatherford Award for Best in Appalachian Fiction and was adapted for the stage in 2016 by Georgia's Historic State Theater, The Springer. She has worked as a journalist for various newspapers around the country and as a guest lecturer at Central Washington University, Ellensburg, Washington.

She blogs at karenzach.com and tweets @karenzach. She is available for book clubs and speaking engagements.

Discussion Questions

1. Did you read *Mother of Rain* and *Burdy* prior to reading *Christian Bend*? If so, what were your thoughts about this final book? If not, did reading this book make you want to go back and read the others?

2. Which of the characters did you relate most to? Why?

3. Which character did you like the least? Why?

4. The author is a Gold Star daughter. Do you think losing her father at a young age to the war in Vietnam informed the story? If so, how so?

5. Why do you think it was Burdy and not Rain who compelled Zebulon to return to the Bend after all these years away?

6. Do you think Maizee would have taken her own life if Zebulon had come home after the war? Do you think their marriage would have held up?

7. There was a time in this country when deaf people had no access to school or tools for overcoming their deafness. Deaf people in that era were considered "Deaf and Dumb." Have you ever heard those terms? What did they mean to you?

8. What changes have you seen in your lifetime toward the disabled? What changes do you think still need to take place?

9. The story of *Christian Bend* is a story about community and redemption. Have you ever belonged to a community like Christian Bend? What was that like?

10.Do you think communities like that exist anymore? What are some of the key components of a good community?

11. Does a person need to live in a rural area to find what the people of *Christian Bend* possess?

12. Guilt and shame kept Zebulon Hurd from returning home, from being reconciled to his own son. Have you ever known the kind of guilt

or shame that Zeb felt? Did you experience the sort of isolation that Zeb encountered?

13. Do you know any war veterans like Zebulon? Men or women who carry the burden of having survived?

14. How can communities better help our war veterans with their Survivor's guilt?

15. Post-Traumatic Stress Disorder isn't something that just affects veterans. Rape victims. Crime victims. Natural disasters. Divorce. Child abuse. Child neglect. All these things can create PTSD. Do you know the signs of PTSD? Have you or someone in your life ever dealt with PTSD? If so, what are some things that helped?

16. In all three books, Rain is the character who loses the most, yet, he's able to reconcile with his father. What made him able to do that?

17. Do you think that forgiveness is a choice we make? No matter the wrong inflicted?

18. Zacharias is an author who writes with a voice toward education and advocacy, even in her novels. *Mother of Rain* deals with postpartum psychosis. *Burdy* deals with Post-Traumatic Stress Disorder. *Christian Bend* deals with guilt and reconciliation. When reading fiction, do you want a story that advocates and educates, or would you rather have a story that simply entertains? Who are some other authors you've come across who employ advocacy in their fiction?

19. Kade often notes the changes that have come to Appalachia due to drug trafficking. The opiate problem in this nation has reached epidemic levels. Some cities are reporting double-digit overdoses on the same day. Have you seen an increase in prescription drug problems or addictions in your community? How is this epidemic affecting your communities?

20. If anyone should know how to help an addict, it should be a police officer, right? Why do you think Chief Conley was unable to help Clive get the help he needed?

21. *Mother of Rain* was adapted for the stage by Paul Pierce, artistic director at Georgia's Historic theater, *The Springer*. Of the three books,

which do you think would make the best movie? Why? Who would you like to see in the lead roles?

22. Zebulon struggles in a large sense with an unforgiveness toward God for the chaos of his life. Have you ever had to forgive God for something? What helped you?

23. Why do you think Burdy was finally willing to marry Clint? What did you think of her asking him instead of the other way around? Have you ever known a woman who asked a man to marry her?

24. There are certain cultures in the world where men take the names of their wives. What do you think of that?

25. What did you learn about Appalachia from reading these novels? Did any of these stories challenge your perception of the region? If so, how? If not, did these stories reinforce your already preconceived notion of the region?

F
Zac
Zacharias, Karen Spears
Christian bend.